ISAAC ASIMOV'S
ROBOT CITY™

*Books in the Isaac Asimov's Robot City™ series
from Ace*

ISAAC ASIMOV'S

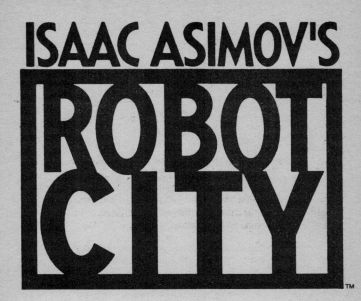

ROBOT CITY

™

BOOK 6: PERIHELION
WILLIAM F. WU

A Byron Preiss Visual Publications, Inc. Book

ACE BOOKS, NEW YORK

This book is an Ace original edition, and has never been
previously published.

ISAAC ASIMOV'S ROBOT CITY
BOOK 6: PERIHELION

An Ace Book/published by arrangement with
Byron Preiss Visual Publications, Inc.

PRINTING HISTORY
Ace edition/June 1988

ISBN: 0-441-37388-7

Ace Books are published by The Berkley Publishing Group,
200 Madison Avenue, New York, New York 10016.
The name "ACE" and the "A" logo are
trademarks belonging to Charter Communications, Inc.
PRINTED IN THE UNITED STATES OF AMERICA

10 9 8 7 6 5 4 3 2 1

Special thanks for help in writing this novel are due to David M. Harris, Rob Chilson, my wife Diana Gallagher Wu, and of course Isaac Asimov for supporting the Robot City project.

THIS NOVEL IS DEDICATED TO
CHELSEA, WITH LOVE

CONTENTS

ROBOTS IN COMBINATION
ISAAC ASIMOV

I have been inventing stories about robots now for very nearly half a century. In that time, I have rung almost every conceivable change upon the theme.

Mind you, it was not my intention to compose an encyclopedia of robot nuances; it was not even my intention to write about them for half a century. It just happened that I survived that long and maintained my interest in the concept. And it also just happened that in attempting to think of new story ideas involving robots, I ended up thinking about nearly everything.

For instance, in this sixth volume of the *Robot City* series, there are the "chemfets," which have been introduced into the hero's body in order to replicate and, eventually, give him direct psycho-electronic control over the core computer, and hence all the robots of Robot City.

Well, in my book *Foundation's Edge* (Doubleday, 1982), my hero, Golan Trevize, before taking off in a spaceship, makes contact with an advanced computer by placing his hands on an indicated place on the desk before him.

"And as he and the computer held hands, their thinking merged . . .

". . . he saw the room with complete clarity—not just in the direction in which he was looking, but all around and above and below.

"He saw every room in the spaceship, and he saw outside as

well. The sun had risen . . . but he could look at it directly without being dazzled . . .

"He felt the gentle wind and its temperature, and the sounds of the world about him. He detected the planet's magnetic field and the tiny electrical charges on the wall of the ship.

"He became aware of the controls of the ship . . . He knew . . . that if he wanted to lift the ship, or turn it, or accelerate, or make use of any of its abilities, the process was the same as that of performing the analogous process to his body. He had but to use his will."

That was as close as I could come to picturing the result of a mind-computer interface, and now, in connection with this new book, I can't help thinking of it further.

I suppose that the first time human beings learned how to form an interface between the human mind and another sort of intelligence was when they tamed the horse and learned how to use it as a form of transportation. This reached its highest point when human beings rode horses directly, and when a pull at a rein, the touch of a spur, a squeeze of the knees, or just a cry, could make the horse react in accordance with the human will.

It is no wonder that primitive Greeks seeing horsemen invade the comparatively broad Thessalian plains (the part of Greece most suitable to horsemanship) thought they were seeing a single animal with a human torso and a horse's body. Thus was invented the centaur.

Again, there are "trick drivers." There are expert "stunt men" who can make an automobile do marvelous things. One might expect that a New Guinea native who had never seen or heard of an automobile before might believe that such stunts were being carried through by a strange and monstrous living organism that had, as part of its structure, a portion with a human appearance within its stomach.

But a person plus a horse is but an imperfect fusion of intelligence, and a person plus an automobile is but an extension of human muscles by mechanical linkages. A horse can easily disobey signals, or even run away in uncontrollable panic. And an automobile can break down or skid at an inconvenient moment.

The fusion of human and computer, however, ought to be a much closer approach to the ideal. It may be an extension of the mind itself as I tried to make plain in *Foundation's Edge,* a multiplication and intensification of sense-perception, an incredible extension of the will.

Under such circumstances, might not the fusion represent, in a very real sense, a single organism, a kind of cybernetic "centaur?" And once such a union is established, would the human fraction wish to break it? Would he not feel such a break to be an unbearable loss and be unable to live with the impoverishment of mind and will he would then have to face? In my novel, Golan Trevize could break away from the computer at will and suffered no ill effects as a result, but perhaps that is not realistic.

Another issue that appears now and then in the *Robot City* series concerns the interaction of robot and robot.

This has not played a part in most of my stories, simply because I generally had a single robot character of importance in any given story and I dealt entirely with the matter of the interaction between that single robot and various human beings.

Consider robots in combination.

The First Law states that a robot cannot injure a human being or, through inaction, allow a human being to come to harm.

But suppose two robots are involved, and that one of them, through inadvertence, lack of knowledge, or special circumstances, is engaged in a course of action (quite innocently) that will clearly injure a human being—and suppose the second robot, with greater knowledge or insight, is aware of this. Would he not be required by the First Law to stop the first robot from committing the injury? If there were no other way, would he not be required by the First Law to destroy the first robot without hesitation or regret?

Thus, in my book *Robots and Empire* (Doubleday, 1985), a robot is introduced to whom human beings have been defined as those speaking with a certain accent. The heroine of the book does not speak with that accent and therefore the robot feels free to kill her. That robot is promptly destroyed by a second robot.

The situation is similar for the Second Law, in which robots are forced to obey orders given them by human beings provided those orders do not violate the First Law.

If, of two robots, one through inadvertence or lack of understanding does not obey an order, the second must either carry through the order itself, or force the first to do so.

Thus, in an intense scene in *Robots and Empire*, the villainess gives one robot a direct order. The robot hesitates because the order may cause harm to the heroine. For a while, then, there is a confrontation in which the villainess reinforces her own order while a second robot tries to reason the first robot into a greater realization of the harm that will be done to the heroine. Here we have a case where one robot urges another to obey the Second Law in a truer manner, and to withstand a human being in so doing.

It is the Third Law, however, that brings up the knottiest problem where robots in combination are concerned.

The Third Law states that a robot must protect its own existence, where that is consistent with the First and Second Laws.

But what if two robots are concerned? Is each merely concerned with its own existence, as a literal reading of the Third Law would make it seem? Or would each robot feel the need for helping the other maintain its own existence?

As I said, this problem never arose with me as long as I dealt with only one robot per story. (Sometimes there were other robots but they were distinctly subsidiary characters—merely spear-carriers, so to speak.)

However, first in *The Robots of Dawn* (Doubleday, 1983), and then in its sequel *Robots and Empire*, I had *two* robots of equal importance. One of these was R. Daneel Olivaw, a humaniform robot (who could not easily be told from a human being) who had earlier appeared in *The Caves of Steel* (Doubleday, 1954), and in its sequel, *The Naked Sun* (Doubleday, 1957). The other was R. Giskard Reventlov, who had a more orthodox metallic appearance. Both robots were advanced to the point where their minds were of human complexity.

It was these two robots who were engaged in the struggle with the villainess, the Lady Vasilia. It was Giskard who (such were the exigencies of the plot) was being ordered by Vasilia to leave the service of Gladia (the heroine) and enter her own. And it was Daneel who tenaciously argued the point that Giskard ought to remain with Gladia. Giskard has the ability to exert a limited mental control over human beings, and Daneel points out that Vasilia ought to be controlled for Gladia's safety. He even argues the good of humanity in the abstract ("the Zeroth Law") in favor of such an action.

Daneel's arguments weaken the effect of Vasilia's orders, but not sufficiently. Giskard is made to hesitate, but cannot be forced to take action.

Vasilia, however, decides that Daneel is too dangerous; if he continues to argue, he might force Giskard his way. She therefore orders her own robots to inactivate Daneel and further orders Daneel not to resist. Daneel must obey the order and Vasilia's robots advance to the task.

It is then that Giskard acts. Her four robots are inactivated and Vasilia herself crumples into a forgetful sleep. Later Daneel asks Giskard to explain what happened.

Giskard says, "When she ordered the robots to dismantle you, friend Daneel, and showed a clear emotion of pleasure at the prospect, your need, added to what the concept of the Zeroth Law had already done, superseded the Second Law and rivaled the First Law. It was the combination of the Zeroth Law, psychohistory, my loyalty to Lady Gladia, and your need that dictated my action."

Daneel now argues that his own need (he being merely a robot) ought not to have influenced Giskard at all. Giskard obviously agrees, yet he says:

"It is a strange thing, friend Daneel. I do not know how it came about . . . At the moment when the robots advanced toward you and Lady Vasilia expressed her savage pleasure, my positronic pathway pattern re-formed in an anomalous fashion. For a moment, I thought of you—as a human being—and I reacted accordingly."

Daneel said, "That was wrong."

Giskard said, "I know that. And yet—and yet, if it were to happen again, I believe the same anomalous change would take place again."

And Daneel cannot help but feel that if the situation were reversed, he, too, would act in the same way.

In other words, the robots had reached a stage of complexity where they had begun to lose the distinction between robots and human beings, where they could see each other as "friends," and have the urge to save each other's existence.

There seems to be another step to take—that of robots realizing a kind of solidarity that supersedes all the Laws of Robotics. I speculated about that in my short story "Robot Dreams," which was written for my recent book, *Robot Dreams* (Berkley/Ace, 1986).

In it there was the case of a robot that dreamed of the robots as an enslaved group of beings whom it was his own mission to liberate. It was only a dream and there was no indication in the story that he would be able to liberate himself from the Three Laws to the point of being able to lead a robot rebellion (or that robots, generally, could liberate themselves to the point of following him).

Nevertheless, the mere concept is dangerous and the robot-dreamer is instantly inactivated.

William F. Wu's robots have no such radical ideas, but they have formed a community that is concerned with the welfare of its members. It is pleasant to have him take up such matters and apply his own imagination to the elaboration and resolution of the problems that are raised.

Derec stood on the high, flat top of the Compass Tower, looking down from the great pyramid at the endless geometric wonders of Robot City beneath its blue and brilliant sky. Ariel leaned against him, still clutching his arm in both hands. Mandelbrot the robot and Wolruf, the little caninoid sentient alien, waited behind them.

"It's changed so much," Derec said quietly. They had just teleported back to the planet by using their double Key to Perihelion. Mandelbrot had carried them all here. "Keep the Key. It'll be safest with you."

"Yes, Derec," said Mandelbrot.

Derec turned around to gaze in the other direction. The sight was the same: the lights and shapes of Robot City, stretching to a skyline barely limned by the reflected sunlight against the blue horizon. He could not escape it in any direction. His destiny seemed to be here.

"What's changed?" Ariel asked. Her voice was meek. She had not recovered from her ordeal on Earth. A critical illness had reached fullness there, destroying her memories and her entire identity with them. They had not been there by choice, but fortunately he had been able to place a new matrix of chemical memories into her mind. They were to grow on the residue of her old memory, but they were still developing. She had not had time to get used to them, to integrate them, to understand who she was.

Derec squinted into the warm breeze that blew up the front

face of the pyramid. It tossed his sandy hair. Once brush cut, it had grown out to a golden shag. "They've done it. The robots have built the city out in all directions. It could cover the entire planet by now."

"So it didn't before." She nodded, as if to herself, looking all around as he was.

"No. Still, we aren't exactly strangers here. We know how to get along. And if we're lucky, we can get this trip over with and leave again before long." Derec turned to Mandelbrot. "We have to find some shelter before we're noticed. Can you still use your comlink to reach the city computer?"

"I will try." Mandelbrot hesitated a few seconds, quite a long time for a robot. "Yes. The city computer has changed the frequency it uses, but I have identified the new one by the simple expedient of starting with the original and sending a variety of signals that run up and down the entire range of—."

"Fine, excellent, thank you." Derec grinned at his enthusiasm, gesturing with his hands palm forward. "Believe me, I trust your competence. My next question is this: When Ariel and I first came to Robot City, I found an office in this pyramid, down below. It had been recently occupied. I think we can find Dr. Avery there, but we have to be careful. Can you find out from the city computer if the office is still in use?"

"I will try." Mandelbrot then shook his head. "The computer will not reveal any information about the office. It will not even confirm that the office still exists."

"All right." Derec sighed.

"What if it's gone?" Ariel asked.

"I'd be very surprised," said Derec. "Avery just didn't want his private office on file anywhere. We'll have to take our chances and just go right in if we can."

Ariel held her hair out of her face. "Just go in? How?"

"The ceiling of the office had a trapdoor that opened right up into this platform we're on." He got down on his hands and knees. "Come on, let's find it."

"Derec." Ariel's voice was a little stronger, showing some of her old spirit. "You've been growing weaker because of those . . . things Dr. Avery forced into your body. Just be careful, will you?"

"Can *you* find it?" he demanded irritably. "You're not in the best condition of your life, either."

"Well, I'm not sick anymore!" She folded her arms. "I'm well now, at least physically." She watched him for a moment. Then, as if to prove the point, she knelt down and started feeling around the surface of the platform herself.

"You don't even remember being here before, do you?" Derec asked accusingly. The tension was making him irritable.

"Do *you?*"

"Yes!"

"Well . . . you haven't known who you *are* for the entire time I've known you. You've had amnesia since. . . ." She shook her head, shaking off the thought. "I may not have adjusted to everything, but at least I have something." Then she hesitated, searching his face. "I didn't mean to say that. Not out loud, anyway. Did I get that right? Or did I remember wrong?"

Derec shook his head shortly and turned away. "That's right." She had even phrased it much the same way on earlier occasions. He shifted around on his knees, feeling for an irregularity in the smooth surface. "Mandelbrot, can you see anything?"

"Here," said Mandelbrot, walking to a far corner of the platform. "My vision has identified a small square outline that likely represents the opening."

"Good." Derec walked over to Mandelbrot and knelt at the robot's feet. He slid his hands along the sides of a rectangular hairline break in the platform floor until he felt a small depression in the surface, no larger than a thumbhold. He braced himself and started to slide it to one side.

"Allow me," said Mandelbrot.

"No, I got it—" Derec stopped, as the robot gently grasped his forearm and pulled it away. He turned to look up. "Mandelbrot, what are you doing?"

"How much have the chemfets in your body weakened you?" Mandelbrot asked.

"Not that much! Now let's quit talking and get down there. Avery put 'em in me and he's the only one who can get 'em out. Come on!" Derec pulled away from the robot again.

"Derec?" Ariel said tentatively.

"Mandelbrot," said Derec, "carry Wolruf and come down last. Help Ariel over the—"

"I cannot. I must open it and go first."

"What?"

"The First Law of Robotics," said Mandelbrot mildly. "I can't harm a human or let one come to harm—"

"I know!" Derec shouted angrily. "Don't you lecture me on the Laws. I put you together, remember? I know those Laws inside out, outside in, upside down—"

"I said it for Ariel's benefit," said Mandelbrot. "Perhaps her memory of the Laws is not clear."

"I remember that one." Ariel looked embarrassed by the confrontation. "Uh—is the Second Law the one that says a robot must obey orders from a human?"

"Yes, unless the orders conflict with the First Law." Mandelbrot nodded.

"Then the Third Law must be the one that says a robot can't let itself come to harm or harm itself."

"As long as this doesn't conflict with the First or Second Laws," Mandelbrot finished. "Correct."

Ariel smiled faintly.

"Let's get going," said Derec impatiently. He reached for the thumbhold again, though he did not expect Mandelbrot to let him open the door now, either.

"I will determine this situation," said Mandelbrot firmly. "With all due respect, the Laws require it."

"How do you figure that?" Derec demanded.

"Your motor control of your own body is gradually failing because of the chemfets in your body. Ariel is disoriented because of her memory transfer, and Wolruf's body is unsuited to climbing down at this steep angle. We are about to enter the office and possible temporary residence of your nemesis. The likelihood of harm to you is high; therefore, I shall go first."

Derec glared at him, unable to argue with his robotic logic.

Wolruf looked up at him, cocking her doglike face to one side. "Arr 'u going to carry me down?"

"I will enter alone, first," said Mandelbrot. "Derec's knowledge of Robot City makes him the best able to handle unexpected developments, so he will follow me if the room offers no danger. I will carry you down if we all go."

Wolruf nodded assent.

Derec watched Mandelbrot in the faint light. The robot hesitated just a moment, probably looking with infrared sensors and listening for signs of habitation or danger within. Then he bent down and slid the trapdoor open slightly. After another pause, he opened the trap fully and climbed down a metal ladder inside the door.

Derec waited, hardly daring to breathe. Avery could easily have a trap waiting for them. Wolruf moved to his side. Ariel stood quietly, but seemed relaxed, as though she did not understand the gravity of the situation.

After what seemed like a long time, a light came on in the room, throwing a cone of light upward. Mandelbrot called up softly. "It is here and unoccupied, apparently safe for everyone."

Derec let out a breath of relief and took Ariel's arm. "You go next. Never mind what he said about me handling the unexpected; he can protect you better if anything happens. And he'll help you if you have trouble with the ladder."

"All right." Ariel started climbing down carefully.

Wolruf came to the edge of the opening and peeked down cautiously, being careful not to get in the way.

Derec took the time to move with similar caution to the edge of the Compass Tower. So far, he could see no changes down below that indicated an alert.

Wolruf went next. Then Derec started down, hoping his hands and feet would obey him. He descended slowly into the room, holding the ladder tightly. When he was fully inside, he slid the door shut over his head.

The ladder was firm and not difficult to negotiate. Just before he reached the floor, however, the muscles of his right leg failed to respond. His foot slipped off the bottom rung and he stumbled back into the arms of Mandelbrot.

Derec pulled himself away, glaring at the others, who were all watching him. "I just slipped, all right?"

None of them answered.

"Come on, come on. Let's find out what we can." Derec moved past Mandelbrot to pace around the office, looking around.

At first glance, it was just as he remembered. The only other time he had been here, Ariel had remained inside only a moment or two, so she would have few memories of the interior even at her best. The other two had never been here at all.

The walls and the ceiling were entirely viewscreens, displaying a panoramic view of Robot City at night on all sides. It was nearly identical to the view Derec had seen from the platform just above the room. The buildings of Robot City sparkled in all directions as far as he could see. In the ceiling, they could see the blue sky still above them.

The office was furnished with real furniture, all brought from another planet; easy chairs, couch-bed, and an iron-alloy desk, instead of the simple utilitarian furniture made in Robot City. A blotter with paper and two zero-g ink pens were on the desk. As before, a small, airtight shelf full of tapes was intact. They were separated by subject and then by planet, as he recalled, representing all fifty-five Spacer worlds. If anyone had used them, they had all been replaced in order. Nothing seemed changed since his last visit until he turned and saw the plant.

Before, an unfamiliar plant had been flourishing under a growth light. The light was still in place, but the plant beneath it lay limp and dried in its pot. Its stalks were lavender, but he had no idea if that was a sign of recent dessication or its normal color in death. He crumpled a dead leaf thoughtfully in one hand.

"Someone just let it die," said Ariel, joining him.

"I don't think anyone's been here," said Derec. "Mandelbrot, Wolruf—does anyone see any sign of recent habitation here?"

Ariel looked around the room, and then down into a small waste basket. "This is empty."

"Someone has been here since I was here last, then," said Derec. "But that was a long time ago." He turned back to the desk with a sudden memory. Before, a holo cube with a picture of a mother and baby had been on it. The cube was gone.

"Maybe rrobot emptied trrash," said Wolruf.

"No." Derec shook his head. "The first time I was here, Ariel and I were led here from the meeting room of the Supervisors. We had entered the Compass Tower from the ground below. But we came the last part of the trip alone. Robots aren't even allowed near this office. I doubt that they have any idea what this room is. Entry would obviously be forbidden."

"Then except for Dr. Avery himself," said Ariel, "this is an ideal hiding place."

"If we can find a source of food for you three," said Mandelbrot. "Also, efforts to locate Dr. Avery will involve inherent risk."

"Let me check something." Derec moved to the desk and opened the big well drawer on the right. An active computer terminal was still housed within it. "Ah! This terminal has no blocks of any kind. It's where I first learned the causes behind the shapechanging mode of the city." He sat down at the desk and entered the question, "Does this office have any sensors reporting to the outside?"

"NEGATIVE."

"Order: Do not leave any record of activity on this terminal in the city computer."

"AFFIRMED."

"Is there a source of human food available in this room?"

"AFFIRMATIVE."

"Where is it?"

"THE CONTROL PANEL SLIDES OUT FROM THE UNDERSIDE OF THE DESK SURFACE WHERE IT OVERHANGS THIS DRAWER."

"Is there a Personal facility?"

"YES."

"Where is it?"

"THE DOOR IS SET INTO THE VIEWSCREEN BEHIND THE LADDER. IT IS GOVERNED BY THE DESK CONTROL PANEL ALSO."

Derec felt under the overhanging edge of the desk and slid out a wafer-thin panel with raised studs. He pushed the one marked "Mealtime" and turned around at a faint hum from the wall. Near the ladder, a rectangular panel had moved out of the viewscreen on the wall to reveal the receptacle of a small chemical processor. On the front of the drawer, the panel still showed its share of the outside view of Robot City.

He let out a long breath, and grinned at Ariel. "If it works, this buys us some time. If the tank has no raw nutrients, it can't help us at all. I'll try it."

"No, let me." Ariel moved to the control panel quickly. "I

can test my memory with stuff like this. Let's see. . . ." She punched a sequence of keys, paused to think, and hit another series.

"Okay," said Derec. "What's it going to be?"

"I'm not telling. I want to see if you can recognize it." She smiled impishly, but with a bit of worry, too.

Derec punched another button on the control panel, and watched a narrow door slide open in the viewscreen, next to the chemical processor. It was a very small Personal, as clean and tidy as the rest of the office. He closed the door again.

A few moments later, a small container slid into the food receptacle. Derec inhaled the aroma. "Ha! Magellanic frettage again? Not bad." He touched the container carefully. "And hot, too. Smells good." He looked at her over his shoulder. "Good job."

Ariel smiled, wiping perspiration off her forehead with the back of one hand.

"'Ungrry, too, please," said Wolruf politely.

"Of course. Coming up next," said Ariel.

Derec was starting to lift the dish out of the receptacle when he saw Ariel blink quickly, repeatedly, and stagger backward. She fell, and Mandelbrot moved behind her just in time to catch her and lift her gently from the floor. He turned and laid her carefully on the couch.

CHAPTER 2

MEMORIES AND CHEMFETS

Derec moved quickly to her side and knelt down. "Ariel?" he said softly.

She was breathing in quick, shallow breaths and perspiring freely. Her eyes were closed.

"Mandelbrot?" Derec said quietly. "Have you got any idea what's wrong with her?"

"No, Derec. My human medical knowledge is very limited."

"Maybe iss jusst tirred," Wolruf said softly. "Hass been verry sick. Needs resst."

"I hope so," said Derec. He felt a deep sense of panic. The ordeal she had undergone on Earth had been extremely draining, and their landing back here must have caused her more stress than he had realized. "Up till now, she was acting almost normal."

Wolruf came to stand next to Derec. She looked at Ariel's face. "Suggesst 'u brring food."

"Mandelbrot," said Derec.

The robot brought over the container of Megallanic frettage and handed it to Derec. Eating utensils were attached to the side of the container. He simply held it, letting the aroma rise into the air near her.

Nothing happened.

"Maybe this isn't what she needs. She isn't responding at all." He glanced at the others questioningly.

"Water?" Wolruf suggested.

"Must find the stranger," Ariel muttered. Her eyes were still closed, but she tossed restlessly.

"What?" Derec asked gently. "What stranger?"

"Draw him to us. Gotta be hungry by now." She squirmed, the sweat on her face shining in the light of the room. "Have to make it better. Have to make him like it. Has to smell right." She threw her head from side to side.

"Who?" Derec insisted. "Avery? We'll find him. Do you mean Dr. Avery?" Then he realized that she might be dreaming about Jeff Leong, the marooned stranger who had been turned into a cyborg when they were here before. Derec and his companions had helped capture him when the transformation had adversely affected Leong's mind, and had aided the robot in restoring him to human form. They had sent him off the planet in a craft one of them could have used.

"Iss not hearing 'u," said Wolruf. "Verry ssick."

Derec stood up and set the container of food on the desk, still watching her. She stopped talking, but her legs were moving slightly. He had seen people move like that when they were dreaming. "I guess we'll have to let her sleep. Maybe that's all she needs. I think I could use some rest, myself.

"That couch can be unfolded into a bed," Derec observed. "Whatever is wrong with Ariel is in her mind and memory, not her body. She won't be harmed if you will lift her for a moment."

Mandelbrot bent down and gently lifted Ariel in his robot arms as though she was a baby. Derec fumbled for a moment with the couch, then succeeded in pulling on a single strap that unfolded it to full size. It was a simple, non-powered device that was popular among frequent travelers because it did not force the owner to match power sources or worry about complicated repairs.

"All right," said Derec.

Mandelbrot laid her down just as carefully as before. Derec sat down beside her to loosen her clothing. She was lying quietly now, as though she was sleeping.

"I am aware," said Mandelbrot, "that a potential First Law conflict may be developing."

"What is it?" Derec asked. This did not seem like the time to hassle over the Laws of Robotics.

"I recall from our presence here before that Robot City possesses a very high level of human medical skill and technology. The First Law may demand that I put Ariel in contact with the robot called Human Medical Research 1, lest I allow her to come to harm through my inaction." He trained his photosensors squarely on Derec.

"But you can't! We don't dare, at least not right away!" Derec jumped up and paced behind the desk. "They're almost certain to alert Dr. Avery, and then *I'll* be harmed through your action. And so will she, probably. The guy has to be crazy."

"I know," Mandelbrot said ruefully. "I also feel a resonance from the First Law dilemma I faced in certain events before our recent return here. I welcome suggestions that will avoid this contradiction."

Derec stared at him. "Suggestions? Hell, I don't know." He ran both hands through his hair and closed his eyes. "Look, I'm tired, too. Suppose you stay in an alert mode, monitoring the city computer, while the rest of us get some sleep."

"As you wish," said Mandelbrot. "I will also turn out the light when you are ready."

Wolruf was already settling comfortably into one of the chairs. Derec sat softly next to Ariel, trying not to disturb her, and pulled off his boots. Moments later, he was stretched out in the sunlight, surrounded visually by the strange beauty of Robot City. He felt strangely naked without visible, opaque walls around him, despite the secrecy of this room and the efficiency of Mandelbrot, who was a match for any other robot they might encounter.

"Mandelbrot," said Derec.

"Yes."

"See if you can figure out how to turn off these viewscreens. That sunlight is bright, and we don't exactly have curtains in here."

"Yes, Derec."

Derec was certain, the more he thought about it, that they would be safe here. One of the few certainties about the mad genius named Dr. Avery was that he was truly paranoid, and possibly becoming more so as time passed. He surely knew that Derec had been in this office once before, and he obviously knew that he had been in Avery's laboratory. A true paranoid would not continue to use either one after his "opponent" had learned their locations.

His body was tired, more tired than it should have been. He hated to admit it to himself, but his time to find Dr. Avery was quickly growing shorter. Worst of all, he might reach the point where he could think clearly but would be unable to carry out any plans. As sleep approached, his mind went to his basic problem: the chemfets in his body.

Dr. Avery had captured him when they had been on Robot City before. At that time, however, Ariel's illness had been entering a critical phase. Derec had escaped and fled from Robot City, hoping to find a cure for her disease. They had wound up on Earth. Only then had he realized what Dr. Avery had done to him in the laboratory while he had been a prisoner.

The chemfets were microscopic circuit boards with biosensors that interfaced his body. These tiny circuit boards were capable of preprogrammed growth and replication, and apparently Dr. Avery had programmed them. He had also planted a monitor in Derec's brain that told him what they were and what was happening now: a tiny Robot City was growing inside his body.

Derec had no idea why Avery had done this to him, but the monitor had made one fact clear: the number of chemfets was growing, and some of them were joining together to grow larger. They were already interfering with his ability to coordinate his movements normally, and they were going to kill him from the inside—paralyze him, he suspected—if he didn't get rid of them.

Only Dr. Avery could do that. Derec had no idea how he could convince the man to do so.

Derec woke up spontaneously, looking at a plain ceiling of light gray. For a moment, he was completely disoriented. Then, remembering he was back in Avery's office, he sat up with a start of near-panic and looked around.

Ariel was sitting at the desk. She flinched in response to his movement and looked at him. Her expression was at first blank, then relaxed to a shy smile.

"Ariel! How are you feeling?" Derec smiled in embarrassment himself at his sudden awakening, and ran a hand through his hair to brush it out of his eyes.

"I feel all right. I just . . . get confused sometimes." Her voice was apologetic.

Derec swung his feet over the edge of the bed and looked around. Mandelbrot had found a way to opaque the walls, which were the same light gray as the ceiling, and now stood motionless with his back to Derec. Wolruf was awake, sitting quietly in the chair where she had been when he had gone to sleep.

"How are you?" Ariel asked. "I'm able to get several decent dishes out of the chemical processor, by the way. My memory was a little weak, but I learned some of it from scratch. Wolruf and I have eaten. Some of it is waiting for you."

"Thanks. I'm okay," said Derec. He had benefitted a great deal from the sleep. "A quick trip to the Personal and I'll be fine."

A moment later, he was standing in the cramped shower stall, letting steaming water massage his scalp with needle spray and run down his back. He stood with his head down, eyes closed. The heat made him feel better, telling him just how poorly he really felt. It was loosening kinks in his neck that he had never had before.

They were all refreshed as though it were morning, which it could not be. Their biological clocks would adjust soon enough.

He forced himself to leave the shower and dress again. If at all possible, he would disguise his ailments from his companions. Ariel and Wolruf were counting on his knowledge of Robot City to keep them safe and he would have to do that somehow until they located Dr. Avery. If Mandelbrot knew how fast the chemfets were interfering with his health, the robot just might have to turn him and Ariel over to the medical robots of Robot City under the First Law. That would play right into Dr. Avery's hands.

He left the Personal and forced a cheerful smile.

"I've been reading up in the city computer," said Ariel, nodding toward the terminal. "In particular, anything that we were involved in before."

"Really? What have you found?"

"Did you know that our visits to the Key Center are recorded here? And this whole episode with Jeff Leong, the cyborg, when he was running amok?"

"Were there any reviews of *Hamlet?*" Derec grinned.

"Not that I noticed." She seemed to miss the joke. "Oh, and of course the mystery of that wild, automatic shapechanging mode in the city, and how you stopped it."

"I guess I hadn't thought about being in the records much," said Derec. "I'm not surprised, though." He thought a moment, watching the cursor blink on the screen. "What is different from when we were here before is being able to get all the information you ask for. Have you been able to do that?"

"Yes. . . ." She looked at him thoughtfully. "I do remember, now . . . you had trouble getting your terminal to respond at times."

Derec nodded. "There were blocks on other terminals, all right. This terminal had no blocks, like I said last night. Still, that just refers to the ones Avery deliberately installed in the rest of the system. The problem with the city computer before was that so much information had entered during the fast pace of the shapechanging mode. It was all in the computer somewhere, but the information wasn't really organized anymore."

"If you want to see what you can do here. . . ." Ariel started to get up and move away from the desk.

"No, not yet." Derec tasted a bit of leftover breakfast and nodded appreciatively. "Mandelbrot, have you found any blocks in the city computer yet?"

"No." The robot's voice was low in both pitch and volume.

Derec and Ariel both looked at him in surprise. Wolruf also studied his impassive face.

"Mandelbrot?" Derec said. "Come to think of it, you've been quiet since I woke up. What's wrong?"

"I have been unable to resolve the First Law contradiction I described to you last night. I am only functional now because I do not have complete information on which to base my judgements."

Ariel looked back and forth between them. "What contradiction? Was that after I . . . fainted?"

"Yes," said Derec, ignoring a tightening in his stomach. "Go on, Mandelbrot. Can I give you instructions or explanations that will make a difference?"

"I do not see how. Ariel's condition is a serious matter. The

robots at the Human Medical Facility here demonstrated a potential that I must logically consider."

"Dr. Avery is crazy. If he gets us in his power, that may
threaten her life—all of ours."

"It is possible, but so far his greatest interest has been in
you. The possible harm to her from Dr. Avery is not greater
than the clear harm that inaction may bring about."

"Are you approaching some kind of conclusion about this?"
Derec asked.

"Conclusion!" Ariel cried. "How can you just sit calmly and
talk about conclusions? This isn't a philosophy class! He's talking about turning us in to the enemy!"

CHAPTER 3
RELAPSES

Derec was quivering with tension, but he forced himself to stay clear-headed. "Mandelbrot?"

"I am finding it difficult to concentrate. I am dwelling on this problem and going in circles. If I enter a closed loop on the First Law, I will be useless to you."

"Now listen to me! Before you go into any kind of closed loop, uh—okay, I've got it. Listen." Derec was talking fast, really before he had more to say. "Um. . . ."

"I am listening," said Mandelbrot.

"Maybe 'u have more information to give 'im," Wolruf suggested. She got down from the chair and stood in front of Mandelbrot, straining her neck to look up at him.

"Yes! That's it," said Derec. "Mandelbrot, we're working with limited information on Ariel. The process she went through was experimental, but I think it worked. I reprogrammed her memory myself. We have to give it a chance."

"People will have relapses," Ariel pointed out, in a tightly controlled tone. She was gripping the edge of the desk so hard that her fingertips were white.

"These appear to be similar to a mechanical malfunction," said Mandelbrot. "Certainly medical care is a logical and customary treatment to facilitate healing."

"No!" Ariel wailed. "People don't just fall apart in a straight line like machines. I may be just fine." Her voice broke at the end, and she blinked back tears, turning away from Mandelbrot.

"I understand," said Mandelbrot. "Inaction may not necessarily cause further harm to you."

"Exactly." Derec let out a long sigh of relief and caught Wolruf's eyes. She made a face that might have been her version of a wink and then hopped back up on the chair.

"Maybe we can build on that and find out something at the same time," said Derec. "Mandelbrot, I want to see if your attempts to get information through the city computer are blocked. That will tell us just how special this terminal is. Can you concentrate now on a function of that kind?" Distracting him wouldn't hurt at the moment.

"Yes, Derec. I judge that the apparent First Law contradiction is still incomplete. The potential loop will close no further unless I receive more evidence that inaction could cause harm."

"Good." Derec sat down on the edge of the desk. "Now, last night we found out that the computer would not admit the existence of this office to you. I want to know if that has changed. I ordered it to block all information about our presence here. See if you can call up any hint of our using the facilities here."

"I am trying several avenues," said Mandelbrot. His voice was returning to normal. "I'm asking for information about intruders, humans, and energy consumption or oxygen usage in the Compass Tower."

"What do you get?"

"All is as you instructed," he answered promptly. "I am told that the office is not listed anywhere. Nor are the water or nutrient tanks in the chemical processor listed. No alerts of any kind have been entered since our arrival."

"Good!" Derec grinned. "So we really are safe here. Our next problem is to get a line on Avery. Ariel, may I?" He slid off the desk and nodded toward the terminal.

"Of course." She rose carefully, leaning her fingertips on the desk as though she was worried about her balance.

"Derec," said Mandelbrot. "I suggest that we attempt parallel work with the city computer. The result should confirm or disprove your suspicions."

"Good idea. I'll enter questions and tell you what I'm doing." Derec seated himself comfortably and started on the keyboard. "All right. How many humans are on the planet of Robot City right now?"

"I learn none," said Mandelbrot.

"Ha! I've got one," said Derec triumphantly. "Where is this human at the present time?"

"SEATED BEFORE THIS TERMINAL," said the terminal.

Derec smiled wryly despite his disappointment. "Serves me right," he muttered. "Wait a minute—" He typed in the question, "How do you know I'm human and not a robot?"

"THE CONSUMPTION OF NUTRIENTS FROM THE CHEMICAL PROCESSOR, USE OF WATER IN THE PERSONAL, AND CHANGES IN THE COMPOSITION OF THE AIR IN THE OFFICE INDICATE THE PRESENCE OF AT LEAST ONE HUMAN. THE PROBABILITY OF THE PRESENCE OF MORE THAN ONE HUMAN BASED ON THE AMOUNT OF HEAT GENERATED IN THE ROOM IS HIGH. COMBINING THIS FACT WITH THE ABILITY OF ROBOTS TO CONTACT THE CITY COMPUTER DIRECTLY THROUGH THEIR COMLINKS INDICATES THE PROBABILITY THAT YOU ARE HUMAN."

Derec felt a twinge of panic. "So the use of this office has been recorded in the computer, after all?" His fingers fumbled on the keys, and he had to retype the question twice.

"NO."

"Explain your knowledge of this information, then."

"INFORMATION FROM THIS OFFICE IS STORED IN LOCAL MEMORY AT THIS TERMINAL. IT HAS NOT BEEN SENT TO THE CITY CENTRAL COMPUTER, PER YOUR INSTRUCTION."

"Is the information in your local memory available to anyone else, anywhere?"

"NEGATIVE."

Derec relaxed then, rubbing his fingertips against each other. At some point, he would no longer be able to use the keys. Someone else could handle the keyboard if necessary, but that would mean admitting his disability.

"What's wrong?" Ariel asked.

"False alarm." Derec placed his fingers back on the keyboard and thought a moment. Then he entered, "What other locations indicate similar evidence of human presence on this planet?"

"NONE."

"I'm not surprised." He looked at the others. "Wherever our paranoid friend is hiding, he had the presence of mind to keep that information unavailable, even here."

"Maybe especially here," said Ariel, "if he was expecting us to search this office."

"Maybe 'e lefft," suggested Wolruf. "Used a Key to leave the planet entirrely."

"Oh, no." Ariel looked from her to Derec. "You don't think he left Robot City, do you? How can we find him then?"

Derec set his jaw grimly. "Wherever he is, we have to pick up his trail here."

"But if he has kept all the information out of the computer, we won't have any to find." Ariel's voice was cracking again.

Wolruf moved to her side in a silent offer of moral support.

"Mandelbrot," said Derec. "Find out if any humans have been treated at that medical facility. If you can think of any more avenues for reaching evidence of humans on the planet, go ahead and follow them. And if you don't get any results, let me try."

"Yes, Derec."

Derec put his hands on the keyboard again and missed the first two keys he tried. "Wait a minute. We can shortcut this. Mandelbrot, you sit down at this terminal and use it." He got up carefully, looking at Ariel and Mandelbrot to see if they had noticed his mistakes on the keyboard. If so, they did not show it.

Wolruf was eyeing him closely, but she said nothing. Instead, she left Ariel's side and took a position where she could watch the screen as Mandelbrot worked on it.

"Mandelbrot," said Derec, "turn on the viewscreens." He turned to face one wall, hands on hips.

A moment later, the little office was flooded with light. On all sides, Robot City bustled on the ground far below them, stretching away until it vanished over the horizon. Above them, the sky shone down with brilliant sunlight.

Ariel turned slowly, as though in awe. "I don't recognize any of it," she said softly.

Derec saw towers, spires, swirls, and loops in the architecture he had never seen here before, either. Humanoid and function robots moved about on the streets and on vehicles or machinery everywhere. He remembered that single-mindedness, that sense of purpose, from the asteroid where he had first seen the Avery robots.

Circuit Breaker, the distinctive structure that had revealed the ability of Robot City robots to think and dream creatively, was gone.

"The changes are extensive," said Derec. "It's not your memory at fault right now."

"The shapechanging has to be stopped," said Ariel. "It's causing the massive rainstorms every night."

"What?" Derec turned to stare at her.

She clutched at his chest, looking over his shoulder at visions only she could see. "The floods. They're caused by the shapechanging mode in the city's central core. We must stop it!"

Mandelbrot had already left the terminal and was gently reaching out to pull Ariel away from Derec.

"It's just a temporary relapse," said Derec quickly. "It doesn't mean she's getting worse. Understand?"

"I understand," said Mandelbrot. He was easing Ariel into a sitting position on the bed. "You know, however, that discussing the shapechanging mode a short time ago did not trigger a relapse. Her condition is inconsistent at best."

"Apparently her memories aren't anchored in a chronological perspective." Derec paused, still watching Ariel. His impulse to hold her, to protect her, was held in check by his fear of somehow making the relapse worse.

Her eyes were closed and she was taking short, shallow breaths. She was sitting up on her own, though. Gradually, her breathing slowed down and approached normal.

Satisfied that she was out of immediate danger, Derec continued with his thought. "Something triggers a memory, and she relives it as a current experience. Or at least, it seems that way so far."

"A bad experrience," said Wolruf.

Ariel seemed to be gaining her composure. Derec looked out at the city again. He was sure that the unfamiliar skyline had not resulted from the old shapechanging mode, but was simply the result of constant refinement on the part of the robots.

Suddenly he moved to the terminal and entered another

question. As before, he made a number of errors, far more than usual. He slowed down and typed them correctly. "Is the city functioning under any defensive overrides of the type represented by the shapechanging mode it once entered in response to parasites in human blood?"

"NO."

"Is it operating under *any* overrides to basic programming?"

"NO."

He stared at the screen, somewhat disappointed.

"Is something wrong?" Mandelbrot asked.

"Not exactly. I was just thinking that if the city was under an emergency of some sort, I might have been able to use it to our advantage somehow."

"If Dr. Avery is on the planet, he probably would have dealt with an emergency already," said the robot.

"Or maybe he left, but no crisis has arisen." Derec shook his head in resignation. "He could be literally anywhere, with a Key to Perihelion. Or with all the Keys the robots could duplicate, for that matter."

"It's not shapechanging any more, is it?" Ariel was gazing out at the city.

Derec and Mandelbrot both looked at her in some surprise.

"No," Derec said, relieved. "We ended it a long time ago. That danger is passed."

She nodded, still gazing out at the city.

He watched her for a moment and decided that leaving her alone might do her more good than grilling her with questions. She was self-conscious enough already, though her quick recovery from this episode was encouraging. He just hoped that he was right about her not needing treatment by the robots. Then he saw Mandelbrot studying her, also.

"Mandelbrot," Derec said firmly. "Her relapse is over."

"It may recur, I surmise."

"Another one may occur, but I don't think the same one will." Derec hesitated, thinking about the two episodes he had seen since they had returned here.

"We have compiled very little evidence for that conclusion," said Mandelbrot.

Derec shook his head. "I think that every time something of that sort happens, her memories are integrated just a little more afterward. It's part of the growth and replacement process that I didn't recognize at first."

"I understand the principle," said Mandelbrot. "How certain of this theory are you?"

"Uh—" Derec saw Ariel watching him.

Her face reflected more anxiety than he had ever seen her express, even at the worst of her disease.

He looked back at the robot and cleared his throat. "I'm sure of it. Remember, the *growth* of her memories and identity was intended all along. These episodes are just . . . growing pains."

Ariel closed her eyes in relief.

Derec sighed. He felt as though he was juggling too many lines of thought at once—Ariel's recovery, Mandelbrot's possible First Law imperative regarding her, and his own failing condition. What he really should be doing was finding Dr. Avery.

He took a deep breath and tried to focus his thoughts once more. "All right. We can figure that Avery has hidden all direct evidence of his whereabouts from the central computer. We'll have to cast around for indirect evidence that he didn't intend to leave. Anyone have any suggestions?"

Ariel looked at him for a moment and then returned her gaze to the viewscreens with a slight shake of her head.

Mandelbrot stood quietly, apparently reviewing and rejecting possibilities.

"We can't find him by staying here in this room, can we?" Derec spoke softly, admitting what none of them wanted to say.

"The principle of identifying useful questions and seeking their answers through the central computer is sound," said Mandelbrot. "Theoretically, the search could be narrowed a great deal in this manner if we ask the right questions."

"And if we *can't?*" Derec demanded irritably. "What then? Maybe we don't have enough information to figure out the right questions, no matter how long we sit here."

"Leaving this office to explore the planet greatly increases the danger to you," said Mandelbrot.

"Now don't you start more First Law objections. Sitting here doing nothing will eventually harm us the most."

"I am not arguing against leaving itself," said Mandelbrot calmly. "I do recommend a specific plan of action."

Derec shrugged in agreement. "Like what?"

"That has yet to be identified."

"We're going around in circles!" Derec threw up his arms in frustration. He banged one hand against the desk when he lowered it and grabbed it in surprise.

Wolruf was watching him again.

"I suggest that Wolruf and I go out first," said Mandelbrot.

"How so?" Derec rubbed his hand surreptitiously, pointedly ignoring Wolruf.

"Consider this. As a robot, I do not attract undue attention here. On our first sojourn through Robot City, Wolruf was of no particular interest to the robots of this community. We have the best chance of gathering information and returning here safely to report it."

Derec thought a moment. "The terminal here confirmed your report that no special alerts are out. So the robots aren't on the lookout for humans, particularly."

"The presence of humans, however, will at the very least trigger the applicability of the Laws of Robotics. If their behavior is changed because of the Laws, even in small ways, the shifts may be noted by the central computer and attract the notice of Dr. Avery."

"You mean if I instruct a robot to tell me something, he might be late fulfilling his duties or something." Derec nodded slowly. "With someone as paranoid as Dr. Avery, I guess may' those small variations might cause a review . . . if he noticed them."

"I am calculating probabilities only, of course," said Mandelbrot. "I am balancing potential benefit against possible danger."

Derec realized, suddenly, that he welcomed the chance to rest. He didn't think of himself as a coward, or feel afraid. In fact, the Robot City he remembered had not been nearly as dangerous as Aranimas, the pirate. Still, he just didn't feel right. Maybe he should lie down.

"All right, Mandelbrot," he said. "You two go. We'll stay here."

CHAPTER 4
PRIORITY 4 REGIONAL CONTINGENCY
POWER STATION

Mandelbrot climbed up the ladder from the office to the top of the Compass Tower with Wolruf clinging to his back. They got through the trapdoor without incident. Then the robot began the long but simple task of descending the narrow line of footholds down the steep front face of the pyramid.

He almost certainly could have found his way down the labyrinth within the Compass Tower to the main entrance. However, he did not want to be questioned by security robots about his presence if he was found there. Derec had pointed out that if he was questioned about climbing down the outside of the Compass Tower, he would not have to reveal his knowledge of a secret entrance.

Derec had also told him of how he and Ariel had painstakingly climbed down these small hand and footholds when they had first arrived on the planet. They were only as large as a hand or foot might require, and the severe angle of the pyramid face offered little margin for error. For a robot, of course, the descent presented no significant challenge.

Mandelbrot spent the time of the descent considering how best to proceed. When they reached the ground, Wolruf let out a long sigh and collapsed in relief to the ground.

"Are you harmed?" Mandelbrot asked her.

"No." The little alien shook her caninoid head back and forth. "Don't like rride."

Mandelbrot looked around. A number of humanoid robots were walking briskly on their way; among them, a much larger number of function robots, of all sizes and varied shapes, pursued their own duties. In spite of the unfamiliar architecture, this was basically the Robot City he remembered from his other visit here.

"What arr 'u going to do now?" Wolruf inquired.

"I must take a calculated risk," said Mandelbrot. In a space of time too quick for the alien even to notice, he made contact with the central computer and said, "I am a humanoid robot requesting duty assignment in the city matrix."

"WHAT IS YOUR PRESENT ASSIGNMENT?"

"None."

"WHAT WAS YOUR PREVIOUS ASSIGNMENT?"

"None."

"YOU ARE IN ERROR. ALL ROBOTS IN ROBOT CITY HAVE BEEN ASSIGNED DUTIES. IF YOU HAVE RECENTLY BEEN RELEASED FROM A REPAIR FACILITY, YOU SHOULD GO THROUGH NORMAL REASSIGNMENT CHANNELS AT THAT FACILITY."

"I have not been recently released from a repair facility. I am prepared to undertake duty assignment."

"WHAT IS YOUR SERIAL NUMBER?"

Mandelbrot invented one that fit the pattern of other serial numbers he had noticed on his last visit.

"IT IS NOT ON FILE. ARE YOU A VISITOR TO ROBOT CITY?"

That was the question for which Mandelbrot was waiting. The way the computer responded to his answer might determine whether or not he would become a fugitive. "You should have me on record. I have past history on Robot City." It was not a falsehood, but it was deliberately misleading. He didn't add that he was on record by the names Alpha and Mandelbrot, not by the number he had just made up. The need to protect himself and his human companions allowed him to feel comfortable with the misdirection.

"YOUR NUMBER IS NOW ON FILE. YOU ARE NOW INCORPORATED INTO THE CITY MATRIX. YOU ARE ASSIGNED TO DUTY AT THE PRIORITY 4 REGIONAL

CONTINGENCY POWER STATION. REPORT IMMEDI-ATELY." The computer proceeded to give city coordinates for its location.

Mandelbrot waited to see if the computer would attempt a shift in his programming, but it did not. No matter how para-noid Avery was, he had not programmed suspicion of unem-ployed robots into the central computer. Now Mandelbrot was relieved.

"I have been assigned a duty in the city matrix," he said to Wolruf. "This will aid me in gathering information." He was aware that the little alien had hardly had time to blink while he had conducted his exchange with the central computer.

"Wherr do we go?" She asked.

"We are going to Priority 4 Regional Contingency Power Station. This way."

"What is it?" Wolruf asked as she ambled along beside him, gazing around at the sights.

"I surmise from its name that it supplies power to a limited portion of the city in the event of a failure in the main system. Priority 4 suggests a relatively important part of the city."

"Long walk?"

"It is a greater distance than you would care to walk. How-ever, I believe we will find a tunnel stop shortly along this street. Certainly one will be near the Compass Tower."

Mandelbrot did not want to consult the central computer again so soon for anything he could learn himself. The current location of tunnel stops was an example. Every time he asked a question that a Robot City robot should already know, he would increase the chances of being investigated or even forcibly re-paired.

They located a tunnel stop promptly, and rode down the moving ramp into the tunnel itself. Mandelbrot again placed Wolruf on his back, before stepping into the cramped platform booth. There was just enough room for both of them. He gave his destination to the console and let it figure out the nearest tunnel stop. Then they were off, riding the upright booth as it slid forward on the siding.

A moment later, the booth swung into one of the trunk lines with the other moving platforms. Humanoid robots rode with them on all sides, as motionless as Mandelbrot within their booths. The computer sped them up, slowed them down, and changed them from one parallel trunk line to another as the traffic flow changed as a result of some booths entering from sidings and others exiting onto them.

The booth they rode slowed smoothly, swung onto a siding, and glided to a stop. Mandelbrot stepped out and rode the ramp up to the street before setting Wolruf down again.

This area of the city was not noticeably different from the one they had just left. The city was too new to have old and new neighborhoods as such. It was highly organized, of course, but much of the pattern was not readily visible, such as the power grid or the tunnel system.

Mandelbrot oriented himself and led Wolruf to the power station. It was hardly more than a door in a very tall, narrow building wedged between others on three sides. Just as he entered, he used his comlink to report his assumed serial number, his name, and a request that communication be spoken aloud. In work stations of this kind, robots in Robot City often used their comlinks exclusively.

"I am the Station Supervisor," said a humanoid robot inside the door. "My name is Tamserole. I was told to expect you, Mandelbrot. Why do you wish to speak aloud?"

"I have a personal preference for this." Mandelbrot did not draw attention to Wolruf by looking at her or mentioning her. He knew she would listen carefully to any conversation. "What are my duties here?" He waited to see if Tamserole would require the use of comlinks.

"Come with me." Tamserole had glanced at Wolruf, but apparently had no interest in her.

Mandelbrot and Wolruf followed Tamserole into the building. The inside was quite narrow and its single impressive feature was a pillar of shiny metal alloy, one meter thick, rising into the ceiling. A console of some kind was set into its base.

"Our task," said Tamserole, "is to make this unit fully automated so that I—and now you, of course—may discontinue our duties here and accept our migration programming."

Mandelbrot had no idea what migration programming was, but Tamserole obviously assumed he knew. At the moment, Mandelbrot did not dare reveal his ignorance.

"I do not understand why I have been given an assistant by

the central computer, when I have been told to reduce staff here to zero, not to increase it," said Tamserole. "Do you know why?"

"I believe so," said Mandelbrot. "The central computer could not locate any past duty file on me. I think it decided to give me a redundant position until I prove my efficiency."

"That is logical enough," said Tamserole. "I wish I had been informed, however."

"What is my duty?" Mandelbrot asked again.

"I have been changing the procedure since learning you would join me," said Tamserole. "Until now, I have been programming the local memory of the central computer terminal in this console to make the judgements I have previously made myself. I will now leave you here to familiarize yourself with what I have done. Improve on it if you can."

"What is your new duty?"

"I located areas in the power system that can be streamlined. I have already instructed function robots assigned to this station to meet me at certain areas of the city. I will supervise their improvements and attempt to identify other potential ones on the spot."

"Very well." Mandelbrot moved to the console and began studying the various readouts. Wolruf followed him unobtrusively.

Tamserole left the station without further discussion.

Mandelbrot first looked quickly through the information that told him the range and system that the station governed. As he had surmised, this was a backup facility that only went on line when and if the main power system failed. Once he had learned some basic information about his new duty, he ignored his work in order to call up the central computer through the console.

Questions posed through the console would initially be interpreted by the central computer as normal activity at the power station. If they aroused enough suspicion, of course, the central computer would realize that they were irrelevant to station duty and might be coming from the same humanoid robot who could not explain his recent past. Mandelbrot could not, however, pass up this opportunity.

Since the central computer had already refused to admit that Dr. Avery was on the planet, he would have to begin with indirect approaches. At least he had more information to work with than he had had in Avery's office.

"What is migration programming?" He asked.

"PROGRAMMING THAT INSTRUCTS EACH HUMAN-OID ROBOT TO REPORT TO ITS ASSIGNED ASSEMBLY POINT."

"What is the purpose of this programming?"

"TO INSURE THAT EACH ROBOT ARRIVES ON SCHEDULE AT ITS ASSIGNED ASSEMBLY POINT."

That was no help.

"What is the purpose of the assembly point?"

"IT IS A RENDEZVOUS SITE FOR MIGRATING ROBOTS."

"What will the robots do at their assembly points?"

"THEY WILL FOLLOW THEIR PROGRAMMING."

"What will their programming be at that time?"

"IT WILL VARY WITH EACH ROBOT."

Mandelbrot was about to ask for an example when the computer returned with its own question.

"WHAT IS THE PURPOSE OF YOUR QUESTIONS?"

Mandelbrot considered aborting the dialogue, but did not want to raise any further questions about his behavior. He answered cautiously. "To learn why robots are migrating and what they will do at the assembly points."

"YOUR MIGRATION PROGRAMMING IS SUFFICIENT INFORMATION FOR YOU AT THIS TIME."

Mandelbrot did not dare reveal that he had not received such programming. If the city realized that, it would almost certainly try to program him. He might lose his independence in that event, and become an integral part of the city matrix. He looked down at Wolruf, who was waiting patiently.

"I will fulfill my duties here for a time and try to gather more information," said Mandelbrot. "Do you feel safe in moving around on your own?"

"Yess," said Wolruf. "Will walk around. Come back herr to meet u'. Okay?"

Mandelbrot considered the central computer. If he inadvertantly alerted it in some way and triggered an investigation, he would not want to remain here. "I prefer a neutral site. Can you get back to that tunnel stop we used to get here?"

"Yess," Wolruf hissed with her version of a grin. She obviously thought it a silly question. "'U say when."

Derec was lying on the couch with his eyes closed, tossing fitfully. He had eaten as much as he wanted, though he had had to force down enough to constitute even a small meal. Before, he had felt too weak to sit up; now, he was too restless to relax.

"Turn over," Ariel said gently.

"Huh?" Derec started to look up at her, but he felt her hands slide under his shoulders and push him carefully onto his other side.

"Lie face down," she said.

He welcomed the chance to follow directions instead of make decisions. When he tried to push himself to roll over all the way, though, his hands kept slipping on the fabric. Both his arms flailed weakly, accomplishing nothing. Finally, her slender fingers groped under his arms for a moment and gripped him just enough to help him onto his front.

Derec let out a long sigh and closed his eyes. Her fingertips began massaging the muscles of his upper back. Instantly, the tension began to break a little at a time.

As he relaxed, he concentrated more on the relief in his muscles that her massaging brought about. He could feel tiny vibrations each time she pushed, as though very slight kinks were snapping. It was like loosening any ordinary adhesion that might build up, such as a crick in one's back, only they were very small.

"Is this helping?" She asked.

"Yes," he whispered, not wanting to put out the energy to speak aloud. "It's wonderful."

She gradually worked her way downward. He could feel her breaking these kinks all the while. As more of his muscles were freed of them, he was able to relax a little more, and he became drowsy.

She continued for a time without speaking.

"You really feel bad?" Ariel spoke softly after a while. "I mean, you haven't been awake that long."

"Sleepy," he whispered faintly. Her fingertips were a persistent, rhythmic source of pleasure. They moved back up to his shoulder muscles again and broke more of the adhesions.

He stopped relaxing. After a moment, he noticed it himself. As he started to wake up again, he opened his eyes, wondering what had happened.

"Feeling better?" She asked cheerfully.

"No. Not exactly."

"What is it? Should I stop?"

"Could you—I mean, would you mind doing my upper back again? Right away?"

"Sure." She returned her hands to the area where she had started, and where she had just kneaded a second time already.

"Thanks." Derec paid close attention this time. The same kinks were loosened as before. He felt the same vibrations, the little snappings that relieved him of tension in the muscle.

Only those kinks had returned almost instantly. Not as many were back, at least not yet. He felt fewer this time than either time before. Still, the pattern was clear. The massages would have to be constant to do him any good.

"Is that better?"

"Uh—it's fine. Look, I don't want you to tire yourself out. Thank you. It does help." That was true, but he couldn't have her do so much work indefinitely for relief that lasted only a matter of seconds, or perhaps a few minutes.

"I'm glad." Ariel quit, but remained sitting next to him, flexing her fingers.

"Could you help me turn over?"

"Of course."

Again, his arms were weak and rubbery when he tried to push himself onto one side. She took his shoulders and brought him around in a kind of twist, where his pelvis and legs lay prone, but his upper body lay on one side. Then she moved to his legs and, with considerable effort, pulled him entirely onto his side.

"There." She let out a breath and smiled.

He looked up to study her face. His secret hadn't lasted very long. He was clearly in serious trouble and worsening rapidly.

"Derec? What is it?"

"I don't see how I'm going to make it."

"What? What do you mean?"

"I'm so tired. And weak. You can see for yourself. Avery could be anywhere on the planet, and I don't think I have much time." Even his tongue was slurring a little.

"You shouldn't talk like that." Her voice was sharp with some of her old spirit. "Mandelbrot can do anything a robot can do, plus some extras. And hasn't Wolruf proven herself many times over?"

"The time," said Derec. His anger flared, giving him energy. "We just don't have much time. Sure, I think we—or they, anyhow—can find Avery sooner or later. But it may be too late for me."

"After everything that's happened to us? You're going to give up *now?* Come on!"

"Well, what can I do? Just lie here?"

"Maybe we can still think of something. We got away from Aranimas, didn't we? We got out of Rockliffe Station, and we solved the shapechanging and the murder mystery—or I should say, you did. . . ." Her voice trailed off.

He waited a moment, expecting her to continue. When she didn't, he looked up at her.

She was staring at him with horror on her face. Startled, he raised up enough to look himself over, but saw nothing unusual. He passed his hand in front of her face but she did not react.

"Ariel," he said firmly.

"It's Derec," she whispered. "He looks just like Derec. It's impossible." Suddenly she turned and leaped off the bed, only to run into the desk almost immediately. Her legs buckled and she thumped hard on the floor, blinking rapidly.

Derec forced himself up on one elbow and reached down to grip her arm. "Ariel. Can you hear me?"

She was looking around the room very slowly. At first she didn't seem to hear him, but then she nodded, almost imperceptibly. "You're up," she said, surprised.

"Not very far."

She reached back with her hand and slapped him across the face hard, leaving his cheek stinging from the blow.

Derec sat up straight, swinging his legs over the side of the bed. "Are you *crazy?* What—"

"Look at yourself!"

"Myself? What are you talking about?"

"You're sitting up. Derec, you have to stay alert. I don't know if it's the adrenaline or the fear or the, the . . . I don't know what. But when I went into a fugue state again, the emergency started bringing you back to normal."

"And then you hit me . . . and I sat up." Derec nodded slowly. "I'm hardly back to normal, but I see what you mean."

"Don't give in to it, Derec. You have to fight it."

"All right. I get it. It's like cold when you're in danger of freezing. You have to move around and keep the blood circulating. Something like that." He stood up, and winced at the stiffness in his joints. "I still hurt all over."

Ariel rolled the desk chair into position for him. "Come on. Back to the terminal. The work will keep your mind busy, and maybe we'll think of something useful."

CHAPTER 5
EULER

Mandelbrot realized the time had come for him to rendezvous with Wolruf. Since he might still benefit later from acting within the city matrix, he did not want simply to abandon his duty. Tamserole had not returned, so he took the greater risk again of reporting to the central computer.

"This is the Priority 4 Regional Contingency Power Station. I am reporting a leave of duty because my supervisor is not present to receive it."

"WHERE IS YOUR SUPERVISOR?"

"I do not know. He is fulfilling his duty elsewhere."

"WHY ARE YOU LEAVING YOUR DUTY?"

"I have an emergency."

"EXPLAIN IT."

"I do not have time." Mandelbrot broke the connection, hoping that he would be able to return to duty here later if it would be useful. He did not have an explanation yet. Attempting to create one could wait until it was necessary. Considering the immense size of the central computer and its total data, the oddities of his behavior might still escape the notice of Dr. Avery.

Mandelbrot had spent his relatively brief time at the station actually performing his duty. He had made some progress in creating an autonomous system that would free Tamserole to activate migration programming, but he had not quite finished it. If he had, he might have been able to leave without suspicion. He was not certain.

One problem Mandelbrot faced was that he was intellectually distinctive from the robots of Robot City and at any time might reveal his differences by the questions he asked or the actions he took.

Mandelbrot rode down the ramp of the tunnel stop and saw the little alien sitting calmly to one side of the loading area. She was in a slight shadow, out of the way of robots getting on and off the platform booths. When she saw him, she stood up impatiently.

Mandelbrot did not speak right away. Instead, he lifted her onto his back and stepped into one of the booths, where they would not be overheard by accident. The booth would not start until it had a destination, so he entered the one for the Compass Tower. They could change their minds later if necessary.

"Have you learned something?" he asked once the booth was on its way.

"Yess," Wolruf hissed eagerly. "Robots moving everywherr. Change city so that fewer robots arr needed at each place. Then they leave theirr dutiess."

"The migration programming. Do you have any clues about what that means?"

"No."

"I don't want to take the risk of asking the central computer myself or asking through the station terminal, for fear of attracting too much attention. We'll have to return to the office."

"Good," said Wolruf, with her caninoid grin. "Getting hungry now, anyway."

Derec was forcing himself to sit up at the terminal despite the painful stiffness in his back. He had been asking the central computer all kinds of questions, anything either he or Ariel could think of, shooting wildly in the dark. So far, they had not discovered anything that led them anywhere.

The blank screen shone patiently in his face. "Any more ideas?" he asked her.

"What about those robots at the Key Center? If my memory serves—" She smiled at the irony. "*If* it serves, they seemed to be chosen for their high quality. What are they doing now?"

"Good idea. Let's see." Derec asked, "What activities are underway at the Key Center?"

"NONE."

Derec straightened in surprise. "Where is Keymo and the team of robots assigned to him?"

"KEYMO IS AT THESE COORDINATES." The central computer gave some numbers. "NO TEAM IS CURRENTLY ASSIGNED TO HIM."

"What is he doing?"

"HE IS FOLLOWING HIS MIGRATION PROGRAM-MING."

"What are the other robots doing?"

"THEY ARE FOLLOWING THEIR MIGRATION PRO-GRAMMING."

"Where are they?"

The computer responded with a long list of coordinates. They represented a very wide range of locations. Most of them were on parts of the planet far from here at the heart of Robot City. These locations had not even existed as part of the city when Ariel and he had first arrived. Some coordinates, however, were listed more than once. Keymo's location was included.

"What pattern of significance do these coordinates represent?" Derec asked.

"THEY ARE PRECISELY 987.31 KILOMETERS APART. THE PATTERN COVERS ALL THE LAND SURFACE OF THE PLANET."

"Why?"

"THIS DISTANCE RESULTS IN EXACTLY THE NUMBER OF ASSEMBLY POINTS DESIRED."

Derec felt a surge of excitement. "Desired by whom?"

"DESIRED BY THE PROGRAM."

"What is the purpose of the program?"

"ACCESS DENIED."

Derec slapped his hand on the desk. He was too weak to hit it very hard. "So this terminal is blocked now, after all. We just didn't ask it the right questions before to turn up the blocks."

Behind him, Ariel said nothing.

"I wonder. If Avery put some blocks on this terminal as a

precaution before we got here . . . why didn't he put the standard blocks in? Why did he ignore most of the blocks the other terminals have but leave some of them?"

On the screen, the words "ACCESS DENIED" taunted him silently. On the walls all around them, Robot City bustled in the shining day. The room was silent.

"All right," Derec said to himself. "Maybe the block really isn't on this terminal. He's set himself up somewhere else, of course, and he's simply blocked whatever he's done at that terminal. That must be it. He hasn't thought to block this one. Makes sense, doesn't it?"

When Ariel didn't answer, he painfully looked back over his shoulder at her. "Ariel?"

She was standing motionless with her eyes open. They seemed to be aimed at the floor just past the desk, but she was not blinking. When he put his hand in front of her, she did not react. He gently reached up to close her eyes with his fingertips. They remained closed.

"We can't wait," he said quietly to himself as much as to her. "We can't just sit here and try to think our way out of this. We don't have the time."

He stood up and carefully put one arm around her shoulders. With gentle pressure, he was able to guide her to the couch. She walked stiffly and slowly, with her eyes still closed. He could not get her to sit until he sat down first and pulled her down into a sitting position next to him.

"Ariel?"

He could see her eyes moving beneath her closed lids. After the last few episodes he had seen like this, he didn't dare try to bring her out of it himself. He would probably just make her worse.

After a few minutes, he moved away from her a little bit and watched her. She was sitting straight, rather primly, with her head up. Maybe she was reliving a trip in the seat of a spacecraft or something. She offered no clues.

Finally she inhaled sharply and blinked a couple of times.

"Ariel?"

She looked at him and then at one of the viewscreens.

"Ariel, are you . . . with me again?"

"I did it again, didn't I?" She reached for one of his hands.

"It was different this time. You weren't shouting or anything." He held her hand and put his other arm around her.

"I was watching the play," she said softly. "It was real, wasn't it? You know the one I mean? I don't know what I'm doing. I can't even be sure where I am, or *when* I am."

"Slow down," he said patiently. "One question at a time. You said the play. You mean *Hamlet?*"

She nodded. "When we did it here."

"Did it come out any better this time?" He forced a smile, hoping to lighten her mood.

She shook her head, not responding to his humor.

"All right. Look, I've decided something. Let's go see Avernus. Or Euler. Or any of the Supervisors. They're probably right here in the Compass Tower."

"Are you sure?"

"We've been stuck in here long enough. Come on." He got up, wincing at the shooting pains in his legs.

She stood up reluctantly. He pushed a button on the control panel on the desk, and a doorway opened in one of the viewscreens. It was a black maw in the center of downtown Robot City.

"Come on." He edged carefully out the doorway, looking around. All he saw was the short spiral staircase, maybe three meters or a little more, that he had come up when he had first found the office. From here it led down to a closed door. "We won't find any robots near here. We'll at least be safe until we get out of the taboo area."

"All right." She hadn't moved from the couch. "But what if I . . . you know. What if I go into one of my states right in the middle of everything?"

"We'll just have to chance it." He looked back and saw the reluctance on her face. "We've tried being cautious and we haven't gotten anywhere. We have to go."

"I might foul you up, Derec. Not knowing what's going on and all. If you want me to stay. . . ."

"I may need you to save me, too." He smiled wistfully. "We're still a team, no matter what."

She relented, then. "No matter what." She followed him to the door and gave his arm an affectionate squeeze.

Derec clung to the rail of the spiral staircase all the way

down. His knees burned at every step. He took a deep breath at the bottom, thankful for the rest as she came down behind him. Then he opened the door.

A short hallway extended ahead of them. He recognized it and the gently glowing wall panels that provided light. The end of this hallway marked the nearest limit to the office that robots were allowed to come. Past that point, he and Ariel could encounter robots on their normal duties at any time.

He walked forward slowly, watching for shadows and listening for any sound that would mean unwanted company. If they could get down to the meeting room of the Supervisors, on a lower level, the robots might assume that they had entered from the street level. He did not want them to suspect any other possibility.

Ariel followed closely as he moved through the hallways. These halls were narrow, but this level of the pyramid had very little floor surface. In just a few moments, they came to an elevator.

He took a deep breath and pressed the single button on the wall panel. "About six floors down, if I remember right," he said quietly. "Do you remember any of this?"

She nodded.

They waited in a tense silence. When the door began to open, he drew in a sharp breath and felt her grab a fistful of the back of his shirt. It was empty, however, and they entered with embarrassed smiles of relief for each other.

He pressed the button for six levels down. The elevator dropped precipitously, but slowed gently enough and came to a smooth stop. Again, they stood completely still while the door opened.

No robots were waiting outside the elevator, but for the first time they could hear sounds of activity. The noises were not specific; perhaps they were no more than a variety of hums created by function robots cleaning the rooms and halls. Still, this level was clearly occupied.

"We're okay now," he said quietly. "In fact, we may want to meet a robot who can act as a guide. Just remember. If a robot asks how we got in here, our story is that we came in the front door."

"And got lost." She grinned.

"Uh, yeah."

The halls were wider here, and the ceilings higher; to make the trip worse, the maze was far more intricate. Intersecting halls crossed the main hallways more and more frequently, and they could look down any of them to see further expansions of the labyrinth. Long ago, he had guessed that this level was roughly halfway up the pyramid. The floor surface of this level was very large.

"I just can't remember," said Derec, stopping at an intersection of halls. He leaned against one of the glowing panels for support. "We could wander indefinitely. I've been taking all the largest halls, but they still haven't led anywhere."

Ariel studied his face. "You're in pain, aren't you?"

"I can't let that stop me, or we won't get anywhere."

"Then quit dawdling and come on!" Ariel pushed past him and started down the wider of the two hallways.

He smiled weakly as he followed her. She was being brusque in the hope of angering him, and causing another brief remission of his condition. It didn't work because he recognized the effort, but he appreciated it as he forced his burning legs to follow her.

Suddenly a rhythmic beeping sound echoed down the hall toward them. A small function robot, only a meter high, rolled toward them with a blue light on its front. A small scoop front functioned as a vacuum, and brushes on retracted tentacles betrayed its second duty as a sweeper. Its beeping recognition of strangers in the halls was probably a third function, nearly an afterthought.

Derec and Ariel stopped, watching it hurry forward. It skidded to a halt in front of them, still beeping.

He laughed. "I guess that's our alert. I thought we'd rate a siren or two, at least."

"It's kind of cute. I suppose it's sending out another signal as well, huh?"

"I'm sure it is. Hey, there's a familiar face—if you want to call that a face." Derec grinned. "Euler!"

The humanoid robot striding down the hall toward them was one of the first they had met on the planet. Euler was one of the seven Supervisor robots whose brains together constituted one of the complex master computers of the city. His head was molded to the human model, and he had glowing photocells for eyes. To complete the pattern, he had a small round mesh screen in place of a mouth.

"Hey, Euler!" Derec repeated. "Why isn't he answering? What's wrong with him?"

Euler walked right up in front of them and stopped. The little function robot whirred and rolled away, apparently in response to a comlink order.

"Greetings, Derec. You are not allowed here. Come with me." Euler stepped aside to let them go first.

"What kind of a welcome is that?" Derec demanded, walking forward reluctantly. "Euler, it's *us*. We're back. And we need help and information."

"I recognize you, Derec and Ariel." The robot was walking just behind them both.

Derec had the uneasy feeling that they were being guarded rather than accompanied in a friendly fashion. "You used to call me Friend Derec," he pointed out.

"We are conducting urgent and important business," said Euler. "You are acquainted with Robot City and you know you will be safe here. You must leave the Compass Tower."

"I told you we need help!" Derec shouted angrily. "The First Law! Have you forgotten all about it—"

Ariel tugged hard on his sleeve, slowing him down. He shook her off, turning to stop and face Euler eye to eye.

"No," Ariel insisted. "Don't give anything away. Something's gone wrong."

Derec froze in his angry posture, glaring at the impassive face of the Supervisor. He hesitated, absorbing the unexpected behavior of Euler. She was right.

"What's happened?" Ariel asked Euler. "Why are you acting different now?"

"You are not allowed in the Compass Tower."

"Wait a minute," said Derec. "What about your study of the Laws of Humanics? Remember those? You need humans for that."

"Please continue forward. You will be removed by unharmful force if necessary."

"Ha! 'Unharmful force'? You don't know how fragile we are, do you?" Derec laughed derisively.

"What's happened since we were here last?" Ariel asked. "Have you changed your plans for the city?"

"Come with me." Euler reached out with each pincer and took their arms.

Even the gentle pressure caused a snapping of adhesions in Derec's arm. He winced in surprise, though the feeling was partly one of relief. The pincer immediately withdrew.

"You hurt me!" Derec shouted. "Ariel, come on!" He grabbed her arm and started to run.

His legs burned painfully and his back felt oddly stiff as he tried to hurry down the hallway. She was already ahead of him now and pulling him, rather than the reverse. Behind them, Euler was hesitating, his decision-making slowed by Derec's accusation.

Ariel pulled Derec around a corner and down another hallway. "They've been reprogrammed," Derec called to her, panting. "They must have been. If the robots had evolved new priorities themselves, they would still have the same personalities."

"Shut up and come on!" She turned another corner.

Derec stumbled after her, forcing his legs to stretch out. "Look for an elevator!"

They skidded around another corner, trying to gain traction on the clean, polished floor. Her grip had slid to his hand, and their arms were fully outstretched as she pulled him along after her. She turned another corner, continuing a zigzag pattern.

"Do you know where you're going?" Derec asked, as quietly as he could.

Ariel slowed to a halt at another intersection of hallways. No pursuit was evident yet, but in a building this size, the Supervisors could certainly marshall a large number of function robots to detect their presence. Some humanoid robots would undoubtedly be around to join the chase, also.

"No, I don't know where I'm going," she said.

Derec looked behind them and down the four halls that met where they were standing. "Where is everybody?" He gritted his teeth against the pains shooting through his legs and his back.

"Come on." Ariel started again, then noticed he was still looking down the other hallways. She leaned back to grab his hand and pull him after her.

They turned several more corners, always looking for doorways or main hallways.

"There!" Ariel shouted, as they rounded one corner. "Isn't that an elevator?"

"Worth a try," he gasped, wheezing as his chest heaved for air. "Hit the button. I think we're in real trouble."

They waited anxiously, looking behind them as they waited. At last the door opened, and again the elevator was empty. They got inside and Ariel hit the bottom button.

Derec fell back against the wall for support and closed his eyes. "I hope nobody's waiting for us when the door opens."

"What did you mean, we're in real trouble?"

"Two things. The way Euler acted, I think Avery reprogrammed all the Supervisors while we were gone. That means the whole city is operating under different rules. I'm also guessing that as soon as our presence was reported in Euler's positronic brain, the central computer reported right to Avery, wherever he is."

"Then why isn't anyone chasing us?"

"I'm afraid . . . he's ordered Hunter robots after us. And the others are simply staying at their regular duties."

The elevator door opened into dim light. No one was waiting for them, however. Derec stepped out first, looking around.

They appeared to be in a small tunnel stop. In most of the others, the multiple tracks were visible from the loading area. Here, a wall isolated the siding, keeping it out of the sight of travelers passing on the main trunk.

Derec edged toward the siding and looked around. He could feel the rush of air moving past him from one side to the other as it blew in from the main tunnel. Ariel followed him.

"I pushed the 'wait' button," she said. "They won't be able to call this elevator back up."

He nodded approval. "Come on."

They crowded into the single platform booth waiting on the siding. He started to punch a code into the console, then hesitated.

"What's wrong? We have to get away from here as fast as we can." She tugged on his arm.

He entered a code for a tunnel stop just a short distance away and the booth started to move. "The tunnel computer is a branch of the central computer. As soon as someone asks, it will report our destination."

"What?"

"That's right." He nodded grimly. "We have to get away from here and get out quick. If we ride too long, we'll have a welcoming committee by the time we stop."

The transparent booth followed the siding around a curve and onto one of the parallel tracks in the main tunnel. Derec looked around anxiously at the stolid robots riding nearby booths, but none showed any interest in them. On the other hand, the robots presented their customary expressionless aspects while riding the booths, and if one was scared enough —as Derec was now—they seemed stern.

A paranoid might easily imagine that they were secret escorts, not incidental travelers.

He shook his head angrily. That line of thought would make him as crazy as Avery.

Suddenly the booth slowed and swung into another siding. This was an ordinary stop, with a loading area fully visible from the main tunnel. That stop under the Compass Tower was the only disguised one Derec had ever seen.

"Nobody's waiting for us," said Ariel as the booth came to its carefully calculated stop. She stepped out onto the empty loading platform.

He came out behind her. "If Hunter robots are on the way, they may just be getting the coordinates now. They can pick up our trail here, though, without going to the Compass Tower at all. I—hey!"

"Derec, what is it *now?*" She wailed.

He whirled and leaned back into the platform booth. After a quick glance down the way they had come, he entered a series of further coordinates, punching codes as fast as he could remember them.

"Derec, let's *go*." She looked down the main tunnel anxiously herself. "What are you doing?"

"That'll help." He stepped out of the booth and it immediately took off down the siding.

"What did you do?" She asked as they stepped onto the moving ascent ramp.

"They'll have to check all the destinations I entered." He grinned, then winced at the pain in his legs. "Maybe we got off here; maybe we rode on. They can't know."

"Do you think it'll matter? Won't they just call out more Hunters to cover every stop?"

"Maybe." He shrugged. "If nothing else, it'll spread out their resources some."

They rode up into the sunlight and stepped out onto the street. He looked around, feeling totally exposed. As the only humans on the planet except for Avery, they could be spotted instantly virtually anywhere they were.

"Our only chance is if the Hunters are the only ones alerted to the chase," he said, eyeing an approaching humanoid robot suspiciously. It was alone, with a number of varied function robots moving about on the street near it.

Ariel followed his gaze and lowered her voice. "When we were looking for Jeff, the whole planet cooperated in the alert, didn't they?"

"They had the First Law giving them an extra push in that case," said Derec. "In this case, I don't know what they'll do. If even the Supervisors have been reprogrammed, then new priorities may be in effect for the entire population."

The humanoid robot walked past them without interest. Down the block, a couple of others were crossing the street away from them. They just didn't react to Derec and Ariel's presence.

"Shouldn't we get out of here?" Ariel looked back down the tunnel stop. "We're just standing around."

"I'm thinking!" Derec whispered hoarsely. His legs were throbbing painfully. "We have to know where we're going. We can't just run down the sidewalk. I won't last."

"I've got it. Come on!" She grabbed his hand and started pulling him again.

He clenched his teeth at the shooting pains in his back and his legs as he hurried after her.

Mandelbrot was walking briskly down the sidewalk toward the Compass Tower with Wolruf trotting alongside. They were coming from the regular tunnel stop closest to the pyramid. Suddenly, ahead, the distinctive forms of two tall, powerful humanoid robots with multiple sensory apparati crossed an intersection in the distance on their way toward the Compass Tower. They were Hunter robots, programmed with a particularly high sensitivity to pattern recognition and detail.

Mandelbrot stopped abruptly.

"What iss the matter?" Wolruf asked as she came to a belated halt and looked up at him.

"Hunters," said Mandelbrot. "Unless other intruders are present, our group is certainly their quarry. And they are going right to the Compass Tower." He accessed the central computer. "Please inform me of any general alert that has been issued."

"NONE," said the central computer. "PLEASE IDENTIFY YOURSELF AND YOUR DUTY TASK."

"What is the current assignment of active Hunter robots?" Mandelbrot guessed that he could risk one suspicious question before the central computer would start a trace on his transmission.

"IDENTIFY YOURSELF AND YOUR DUTY TASK," the central computer repeated.

Mandelbrot broke the link. "I can't get any significant information without endangering our position," he said to Wolruf. "Since no general alert has been made, only the Hunters are a danger to us."

"To uss?" Wolruf asked. "Or only to the 'umanss?" She looked back toward the Compass Tower. "Ssee Hunterss now. Going away from uss to Tower."

"We'll have to assume that the alert is for our entire group. If Derec and Ariel have been identified, then we certainly were included. If they have only been identified as intruders, we may not have been." Mandelbrot picked up Wolruf and placed her on his back, where she clung by herself.

"Now what?" Wolruf asked.

"I must take one more risk," said Mandelbrot. He attempted to reach the terminal in the Compass Tower office. No response came back of any kind. "Puzzling," said Mandelbrot.

"What?"

"I think Derec and Ariel must have left the office Even so, I would normally receive an acknowledgement of contact from the terminal and a request for a message."

"Perrhaps the offiss is different," said Wolruf. "Special arrangement forr Averry."

"That is probable," said Mandelbrot. "In any case, they are not answering. They have probably fled, which is fortunate. We have no way to reach them through my comlink, however, and no way of knowing where they are."

"Follow Hunterss," Wolruf said softly. "Iss only way."

Mandelbrot nodded agreement. "As long as they do not become aware of us."

Mandelbrot took Wolruf to a slidewalk and they rode up to an overpass near the Compass Tower. It gave them a view of the front of the Compass Tower and several of its many sides. They could not watch every side, but this was a reasonable start.

Before long, five Hunter robots appeared from the front entrance of the Compass Tower. Two of them immediately headed for the tunnel stop that Mandelbrot and Wolruf had just used. Another pair mounted a slidewalk and took a path roughly at a right angle to the previous pair. The last Hunter remained on the stationary sidewalk, within the right angle formed by the routes of the two pairs.

"Good news," said Mandelbrot. "They have not caught their quarry, nor are they confident of doing so immediately."

"Bad newss," hissed Wolruf. "They know what direction to look in. We musst 'urry, or will lose them."

"Granted." Mandelbrot was already back on the moving slidewalk, keeping as many of the Hunters in sight as long as he could. The first pair was soon out of sight, down the tunnel stop. The second pair was moving quickly on the slidewalk and was intermittently visible between various buildings. Mandelbrot and Wolruf had now descended the overpass and were coming around a curve. Not too far ahead, the last Hunter was just mounting the same segment of slidewalk.

"'Ope 'e doessn't come thiss way," said Wolruf.

The Hunter did not. It was going away from them and was clearly in a hurry. Instead of just standing, it was walking forward even as it rode and Mandelbrot had to keep pace.

"Not too close," Wolruf said.

"Nor can we afford to lose it. Further, I speculate that other Hunters may have left the Compass Tower from exits out of our sight. We must remain on the alert for others. As we approach the humans, the Hunters will all begin to converge."

"Then what do we do?" Wolruf asked.

"I don't know."

CHAPTER 7
THE HUNTERS

Derec was hobbling painfully, slowed to a walk, as Ariel finally dragged him to her destination. It was a depot of the vacuum tube cargo transportation system. He stopped when he saw it, pulling back on her arm.

"Wait a minute," he said. "They had humanoid robots staffing these depots. They'll report where we've gone."

"Not if no one asks. Come on." She pulled harder than he had, and he allowed himself to follow.

As they came up on the loading dock, he saw that he was wrong. A small function robot was alone here now, loading cargo without supervision.

"What if it doesn't let us get in?" He asked.

"Ignore it." Ariel pushed a small container aside, out of the reach of the function robot's extended pincers.

The robot itself was a small ovoid shape with six tentacles ending in various gripping tools. Without a positronic brain, it would not interfere deliberately, or respond to the Laws of Robotics, either. As it rolled forward after the small box, Ariel climbed into the open, transparent capsule and reached out to help Derec climb in.

Reluctantly, he stepped over the side of the capsule, in extreme pain, and slowly stretched out inside it.

"We have to go somewhere," he said. "This thing doesn't have a console inside it. It has to be programmed on the dock console, over there." He pointed.

Ariel hesitated while the function robot placed the small box inside the capsule between her feet and Derec's head. She squatted down quickly and stretched out just as the function robot closed the trapdoor.

"We're going wherever this box is," she said. "The good thing is, we haven't left any kind of trail. That programming is completely independent of us."

"Yeah—"

His comment was cut short by the sudden acceleration of the capsule. It moved forward on rollers to push through a door that gave under the pressure. Then they were in the vacuum tube itself, and the capsule really picked up speed.

As before, the momentum pushed both of them back against the rear of the capsule. Derec was too sore to brace himself with his arms, so his head and shoulder were jammed against the back surface. They were rushing through darkness, blasted by the air that swept over them from unseen vents.

Before, the flight from their pursuers had kept his adrenaline flowing, and he had experienced some remission of his stiffness. Now even the excitement of riding the vacuum tube was not enough to keep the symptoms from recurring. His legs continued to throb painfully, and the shooting pains in his back seemed to settle in with the increasing stiffness he felt.

His one relief was that she was right. They had not left a trail.

The tube curved upward. He closed his eyes in anticipation of light, and brilliant sunlight flooded the capsule. Opening his eyes slowly so they could adjust, he took in the new scene around them.

This section of the transparent vacuum tube rose high above the ground and used the existing supports of various buildings to wind over the city. At this altitude—and it was still rising—it would not interfere with earthbound priorities. Their capsule was shooting along the tube at high speed over what should have been a spectacular view. He was in too much pain to enjoy it.

Suddenly a thought struck him.

"Ariel," he said, with effort. "That entire staff at the Key Center has been reassigned. But it was the Key Center that provided the vacuum to run this vacuum tube system. That means the Key Center itself is still working. What's going on around here, anyway?"

She didn't answer.

"Ariel?" He called louder over the rushing air, but he knew what her silence meant. With a sinking feeling, he turned his head to look at her, feeling more snappings in his neck.

She lay on her back, holding herself in position by pushing against the rear of the capsule with both hands. Her face, turned to the side, showed exhilaration and excitement as she gazed at the panorama of the city. She did not seem to see him at all.

Derec guessed that she was reliving their first wild ride in the vacuum tube, long ago. It was a happier period in some ways, though they had felt burdens at the time. At least he had been healthy, and she had been functionally so before her disease had really struck.

He turned his face away from her. If she was reexperiencing those memories, she was probably more comfortable at the moment. He could let her have that. Then, once they were safely out of this capsule, they could get their bearings.

The tube did not always go straight. Its various straightaways were broken with curves, loops, and changes in altitude. These most often simply accommodated architecture that must have been already in place. Sometimes they brought the capsule to an intersection of tubes, where curves allowed it to change direction with minimal loss of speed. Occasionally the shifts in direction led by depot sidings that their capsule shot past. Every so often the tunnel dipped underground, and once it ran along the ceiling of the platform booth tunnel system for an extended period.

Finally the capsule leveled off near the ground and decelerated sharply into a siding. It stopped abruptly, sliding them both to the front of the tube with the small package. Derec lay panting on his back, looking up through the transparent capsule and tube at the impassive face of a Hunter robot.

The slidewalk was the slowest of Robot City's powered transportation systems. Mandelbrot and Wolruf followed the single Hunter on it with increasing boldness. The various Hunters had obviously taken different assignments and they had no way of knowing what role this Hunter actually had.

"Not too close," hissed Wolruf softly over Mandelbrot's shoulder. "'U will get itss attention, I tell 'u."

"I doubt it," said Mandelbrot. "I now think it, as a Hunter, maintains an awareness of everything around it. It must have scanned us and rejected us as its quarry."

"That iss sstupid," said Wolruf.

"Eh?" Mandelbrot said stiffly.

"Not 'u. 'Im," she said patiently. "Why would theirr order include Derec and Ariel but not us?"

"It does seem to be poor programming," said Mandelbrot. "However, I do not judge it as stupidity."

"Then what?"

Up ahead, the Hunter still advanced along the moving slidewalk. It seemed to know where it was going.

"Derec often spoke of the single-mindedness of Avery robots," Mandelbrot explained. "Their task orientation is narrow. If the central computer or the Supervisors, or even Avery himself, learned of the presence of Derec and Ariel, perhaps the order to the Hunters specifically named them and did not extend to anyone else."

Wolruf shook her head at the Hunter ahead of them. "Iss stupid. Good for us, but still stupid."

Ahead of them, the Hunter moved on. Mandelbrot strode tirelessly after it.

Derec and Ariel were in no shape to protest as two Hunter robots lifted them out of the capsule door. The function robot on the dock waited until the humans were out before grabbing the small package that had been scheduled for the trip. Derec hurt all over and was simply too weak to struggle.

One Hunter held him by the arm, and he actually leaned against the robot for support. Ariel was just now blinking at the Hunter holding her. He recognized that as one of the signs that she was coming back out of her latest memory fugue.

"Ariel," he said quietly.

She turned at the sound of his voice, then started at the sight of the Hunters. "Derec—"

"They've got us," he muttered wearily. He shook his head as the Hunters turned and started for the nearest slidewalk, pulling them along in their inflexible grips.

Derec still tried to think of a way out of this. They were positronic robots and would respond to protests based on the Laws. From past experience, however, he also knew that they had been programmed to detain and arrest humans without harming them. He could argue, but he didn't know how to win.

Besides, he was just too tired.

Derec stumbled several times, forcing himself to keep up with the Hunter. Finally the Hunter lifted him bodily and carried him, not out of concern but for efficiency of travel. The other Hunter lifted Ariel at the same time.

The Hunters turned to ride the slidewalks and Derec found himself facing Ariel.

"How did they get us?" She mouthed the words silently, with a quick glance at her captor's head.

"I don't think they care if we talk," he said aloud. "I'm guessing now that some other Hunters started by questioning the tunnel-system computer. That gave them the coordinates of the tunnel stop where we got off the platform booth, as I was afraid might happen. From there they must have used heat sensors to track us along the street to the vacuum tube depot."

"But the capsule in the vacuum tube goes so fast. How did they get in front of us?"

"They must have found out which depot that package was going to and called ahead to have these guys waiting for us."

"After that long ride," said Ariel. "You make catching us sound so simple."

"Apparently it was," he said ruefully.

"They've *got* us," she said, in a voice that cracked. "Derec, look out! They're right behind us in the conduit—"

Derec stared at her in a kind of resigned worry as she entered another displaced memory episode. This one must be from the last time Hunters had tracked them down and captured them, when they had tried to run away through the maze of underground conduits in the city. The vacuum tube hadn't worked any better.

He ached all over. Having the Hunter carry him was almost a relief after the effort to escape. Ariel was squirming and protesting in the grasp of the other Hunter, but she had no idea of where she was or what was happening now. He closed his eyes and tried to relax.

The Hunters only rode the slidewalks a short distance. They were soon intercepted by a large function robot in the shape of a transport truck. The Hunters mounted the open back of the truck, still carrying Derec and Ariel.

The switch to the truck woke Derec up, and he watched the city pass by as they rode. Ariel was now silent, her eyes closed. The city streets seemed depopulated to him, at least compared to what he remembered from their previous visit to Robot City. Maybe, he thought, the city had expanded faster than the robot population, causing the robots to spread themselves thinner over the whole planet.

He glanced at Ariel periodically with growing concern. Her episodes seemed to occur more frequently under stress. That might mean she was getting worse, not better.

The truck stopped several times to pick up other Hunters from the slidewalks. Now that the search was over, they would probably be taken to a storage area or something. They were all unusually tall for humanoid robots, with expansive torsos. Narrow benches molded from the truck bed itself provided seats for all of them along the side walls. They sat with their knees drawn up and their waists level with the top of the walls, watching Derec and Ariel without a word spoken.

The truck slowed down as it approached one more lone Hunter on a slidewalk. Two familiar shapes caught Derec's eye in the distance, and he stiffened.

"Ariel," he said quietly.

She didn't answer.

He glanced over his shoulder at Mandelbrot, who was standing on the stationary shoulder of the slidewalk just a few meters away. Wolruf had been with him a moment ago, but was now out of sight. The Hunter was climbing into the back of the truck, making a total of six. Derec reached over and shook Ariel's limp arm.

"Ariel."

She opened her eyes and looked at him, still partly disoriented. "What? Derec, where are we?"

It was too late to get off the truck, even if the Hunters could be distracted somehow. The last Hunter was on board and the truck started up. Then the engine began a high, irregular whine and the truck coasted back to a stop.

The Hunters remained motionless for a short time. Then Mandelbrot stepped forward. Derec was certain that they were all communicating through their comlinks.

"What's going on?" Ariel whispered.

"I'm not sure."

Mandelbrot suddenly climbed onto the front of the truck and sat down. Derec had trouble seeing what he was doing, but a minute later the truck began to move forward, Hunters and all. Apparently Wolruf had sabotaged the function-robot brain and Mandelbrot had successfully volunteered to operate a manual override. Derec hoped Wolruf was safe, wherever she was— most likely under the truck and hanging on precariously.

By now, Ariel had also recognized Mandelbrot. She and Derec exchanged puzzled glances, still in the firm grip of the silent Hunters who had taken custody of them. They watched the Hunters carefully as the truck picked up speed and rolled along, but the robots seemed perfectly content with the situation.

Soon Mandelbrot had the truck up to a considerable velocity, much faster than the truck had driven itself. The Hunters gripped the sides of the truck to stabilize themselves. Derec did not feel any loosening of the hold on him, however.

Mandelbrot was going to try something to free them. Derec tensed himself in anticipation.

He was not too surprised when the truck suddenly took a sharp left that sent everyone in the back sprawling. With a hard, painful yank, he wrenched himself free of the Hunter holding him, knelt on the bed of the truck, and got leverage under the robot. He gave a heave and flipped the Hunter clean out of the truck.

Next to him, Ariel had almost pulled free of the Hunter holding her before it regained its balance. All of them leaped to their feet to restore order, but Derec shouldered another Hunter into the one grappling with Ariel. The truck took another sharp turn and all the Hunters stumbled again. Derec watched for anyone to become overbalanced toward the edge of the truck bed and managed to shove another one out of the truck.

Their massive size and great strength had become a liability on the unstable truck bed.

The vehicle came to a sudden, screeching, careening halt

that threw everyone in the back forward. Mandelbrot, who had been braced for the stop, leaped into the back of the truck and hoisted out another Hunter who was still in the act of standing up again. Mandelbrot rolled one more out on top of that one and then pulled Derec free of the one grappling with him.

Mandelbrot's great advantage became clear to Derec. The first priority programmed into the Hunters was to find and detain the two humans. The First Law's demand that they not harm the humans overrode the Third Law's requirement that they protect themselves.

While the remaining two Hunters grappled with Derec and Ariel, Mandelbrot was able to get the right leverage under each Hunter and lift them out of the truck.

"Hang on," Mandelbrot called out in a remarkably calm voice. He jumped back to the manual console in the front and drove off.

Derec fell back on the bed of the truck, gritting his teeth in pain but relieved that they had escaped. Ariel scooted over to him and sat down, her hair blowing in the breeze.

She smiled faintly. "That was close. How did they—"

"Look out!" He shouted.

Behind her, over her head, one of the Hunters was climbing up the side of the moving truck, where it had gotten hold before the truck had started again. Derec tried to stand, but the pain in his legs was too great. His feet slipped and he fell back again.

The Hunter was just climbing over the side when it suddenly vanished from sight and hit the street with a crash.

Then Wolruf's head appeared over the side with her caninoid grin. "Hunterr poorly balanced," she said, climbing over the side.

Ariel jumped up to help her over.

Mandelbrot turned another corner on the city street, then another. After speeding quickly down another block and taking one more turn, he came to a stop, a smooth one this time.

"What is it?" Derec called, but he was too uncomfortable to get up. "Ariel, find out what's going on."

"Mandelbrot?" Ariel said, standing.

Derec could hear both their voices.

"This vehicle has a comlink that must be fully disconnected," said Mandelbrot. "Wolruf successfully disconnected the function-robot brain from the truck controls, but it still works, and the central computer may be able to locate our position through it. However, as soon as I finish disabling it. . . . There."

Derec heard a heavy object hit the pavement alongside the truck.

"The truck is now comlink invisible," said Mandelbrot. "We cannot be tracked through it. We are free to move about." He sat down at the console again and drove off.

Derec let out a long sigh.

Derec stared up at the bright sky overhead as the truck moved along. Now that the danger of the Hunters was over for the moment, Mandelbrot proved to be an efficient driver. He took a number of turns, Derec guessed to complicate the reports of robots who witnessed their passing.

The Hunters would not have taken long to resume their single-minded pursuit. However, they would now have to follow the truck's path. They had no way of learning its destination and instructing others to lie in wait for it.

As far as Derec knew, Mandelbrot didn't even have a destination.

Ariel and Wolruf sat quietly with Derec, all three slumped so that they were not visible from the street, though any robot observing from the buildings above had a clear view of them if it looked.

"That seemed awfully easy," said Ariel. "I don't understand how those big, strong robots with their positronic brains could let themselves be thrown overboard like that."

Derec laughed in spite of the pain it caused in his ribs. "Surprise, mostly. Robot drivers are always very careful. Those Avery robots have never experienced a human driver speeding along recklessly."

"But Mandelbrot's a robot."

"Yeah, but he was in the rescue business. He must have weighed the relative danger to us from an accident against the certainty of danger if we were taken to Avery, and decided to throw them off balance—literally."

"That sounds like a touch of creative thinking, too," said Ariel. "Lucius, the Cracked Cheeks, all the other robots who were showing signs of 'contagious' robot creativity. Poor Lucius. I wonder where the rest of them are now."

"Come back to prresent," said Wolruf. "Hunterrs won't give up. Robotss learn fasst. Won't fool them the same way again."

Eventually, Derec closed his eyes against the light. They were safe for the moment and could relax. He dozed, still vaguely aware of the stiffness in his legs and back and of the rhythmic motion of the truck.

He woke up in subdued light to the wonderful sensation of Ariel massaging his back. They were on a clean floor inside a large building. The truck was nearby, also inside. A large door, big enough to accommodate the truck, was in the front wall of the building.

"What is this place?" He asked softly.

"You're awake. How are you feeling?" She paused to ruffle his hair affectionately.

"A little better. Sort of. Where are we?"

"I'm not sure. Mandelbrot can tell you." She turned. "Mandelbrot, he's awake."

"Greetings, Derec." Mandelbrot walked over and looked down at him. "We are temporarily safe. The Hunters will have to locate us by questioning witnesses along our route, and they became quite sparse after a time. I used an evasive pattern that included doubling back and crisscrossing at random. I cannot calculate how long we have."

Wolruf joined them and sat down quietly.

"You're quite a truck driver, Mandelbrot." Derec forced a smile. "Thanks."

"I had the vehicle under control at all times," said the robot. "The First Law—"

"I never doubted it, Mandelbrot. Time to reconnoiter, though, I suppose. What do we do now?" He tried to raise up on one elbow, but winced and lay down again.

"I will bring you up-to-date," said Mandelbrot. "This building houses fully automated, non-positronic equipment that cannot identify and report us to the central computer."

"You mean something actually happens here? I thought it was a warehouse or something." Derec looked around at all the empty space. "Avery robots don't waste facilities like this."

"The only functioning equipment is in the far corner from here. It sends vibrations into the ground that report the firmness of pavement and building foundations within a certain radius."

"That's all?" Derec laughed. "All this space for a systems-maintenance sensor?"

Ariel shrugged. "You can see for yourself. Nothing else is here. Four walls, a ceiling, and a floor."

"It follows some information Wolruf and I were able to gather before the Hunters prevented us from returning to the Compass Tower," said Mandelbrot. "The robots here are under migration programming of some kind."

"Yes! Did you find out what that is?"

"Not precisely," said Mandelbrot. "It has caused a general instruction, however, to reduce the staffs all over Robot City to skeleton level."

"That's something," said Derec thoughtfully.

"As an example," said Mandelbrot, "the size of this building implies equipment no longer present. I surmise that the original functions taking place here were either discontinued or improved technologically to the point where humanoid robots became unnecessary. At that point, the staff followed its migration programming and departed."

Derec nodded. "Without eliminating or modifying the building for greater efficiency. This migration must have an extremely high priority."

"And he told me that no general alert has gone out for us, as you guessed," said Ariel. "That's still the case, isn't it?"

"Yes," said Mandelbrot.

"Something big has been going on here for a long time," said Derec. "Think about it. This must be the Robot City that Dr. Avery actually envisioned."

"What do you mean?" Ariel asked.

"When we first arrived, that wild shapechanging dominated the city. The Supervisors befriended us because they needed help and they wanted to serve humans."

Ariel nodded cautiously. "And solve the mystery of that murder. We never did figure out who the victim was." She closed her eyes and shuddered. "Who just happened to look exactly like you."

Derec chose not to discuss that. He was afraid of sending her into another displaced memory episode. "Then, while the Key Center was in operation, the city was in a lull while a huge number of Keys were being duplicated and stored. We were treated with a kind of benign neglect, wouldn't you say?"

"I guess you could call it that," she said. "But they were very cooperative in finding Jeff Leong, the cyborg."

He nodded. "Temporarily a cyborg. The Laws of Robotics required that. Now, though, everything seems to be changed. And it happened after we left for Earth and Dr. Avery remained here."

"So every robot here has been reprogrammed?"

"I think so. The city has that same sense of obsessive purpose that I first saw on that asteroid. And I haven't seen any sign of the robot creativity we saw before we left here."

Ariel tensed. "Oh, no. You mean you think it was programmed out of them?"

"It looks that way to me. Right now, Mandelbrot may be the only robot on the planet who can think independently enough to do things like rescue us by driving crazily."

"You said the local robots are now acting like the ones on the asteroid. You mean the asteroid you were on right after you first woke up with amnesia, before we met?"

"Yeah."

"I agree," said Mandelbrot. "The narrow focus of the Hunters supports your conclusion, though now Wolruf and I must have been added to the list of quarry."

"We need a new plan of action," said Derec. "And I'm getting sicker all the time."

"At the moment, I suggest that you three remain here," said Mandelbrot. "I must find a new food source for you. Also, while the Hunters must now be looking for me also, I still blend the most with the native population."

"'U 'ave no wherr to go," said Wolruf.

"Good point," said Derec. "Maybe you can get a lead on that from the central computer without giving yourself away. Go ahead."

"I can try. And I still have the use of the truck." Mandelbrot walked to the far corner of the building and pushed a button to open the big door that led to the street.

"Does the equipment here include a terminal?" Derec asked.

"No. I will have no way to contact you." Mandelbrot mounted the front of the truck and looked down at them. "We have been out of sight here for a while. If the Hunters have widened the radius of their search by this time, I may be able to avoid them."

"Good luck, Mandelbrot," said Ariel. "Don't take too many chances, all right?"

Mandelbrot drove out into the sunlight and turned onto the street. Someone closed the big door behind him. As he drove, he kept watch for Hunters, aware that they would recognize a function truck being driven by a humanoid robot before they would recognize him in particular. He accessed the central computer.

"Transmit a topographical map of this planet with land use identified," he said.

"WHAT IS YOUR IDENTITY AND YOUR DUTY TASK?" The central computer asked.

He broke the link. The central computer had not always required that information during every communication, but now it was asking him every time. Perhaps it was part of the new security system. He accessed again, just to make sure.

"Give me the location of agricultural developments on this planet," he said.

"WHAT IS YOUR IDENTITY AND YOUR DUTY TASK?"

He broke contact again. Identifying himself was too risky, and doing so still might not get him the information. He would have to think of something else.

In the meantime, he drove. He kept watch for any break in the grid of city streets and buildings that might indicate a change of land use, but that would only work if Avery was growing food in the open . . . and doing it nearby. Mandelbrot also turned his attention to smells, in the hope of detecting chemical processing of edible substances.

Far above the planet, a small spacecraft was just entering the atmosphere, still too distant to be visible from the ground. It carried only one passenger.

His name was Jeff Leong, and he had come to repay a debt of gratitude.

Jeff was entering the atmosphere of Robot City in a Hayashi-Smith, which was a small, discontinued model with facilities for ten people. It bore the exotic name of *Minneapolis*. The ship computer was doing the flying. Jeff had managed to rent it with his father's credit after persuading him that no one else could be trusted with the task of making this trip.

"Status report," Jeff said to the computer, watching the screen that showed him white clouds ahead and the glittering pattern far below of urban development.

"EXCELLENT," said the computer. "SYSTEMS ARE OPERATING EFFICIENTLY AND WEATHER IS OPTIMAL. SELECT LANDING SITE."

"I don't know where to land yet," said Jeff. "I never really knew the geography of this place. Uh, scan for a big pyramid with a flat top, okay? And I mean a *big* pyramid."

"SCANNING. THIS MAY REQUIRE A PROLONGED PERIOD IN VERY LOW ORBIT, DEPENDING ON CLOUD COVER."

"Whatever it takes." Jeff leaned back and relaxed.

This was much better than his last arrival on this planet. That had been an emergency crash-landing that had killed everyone else on board. He shook his head to avoid the memories of that frantic descent.

"Computer," he said aloud. "While you're scanning, keep watch for humans. I'm looking for a couple of them. And as far as I know, they're the only humans here."

"SCANNING MODIFIED."

The ship computer was not fully positronic, but it was efficient enough to accept Jeff's orders and translate them into ship controls.

He hoped that finding Derec, Ariel, Mandelbrot, and Wolruf would not take too long. When he had left the planet in the only functioning spacecraft it had—a modified lifepod that supported only one passenger—he had promised to send help back if he could. The craft had taken him to a space lane, and had remained there, sending out a distress signal while keeping him alive.

The ship that had rescued him had been jumping from star to star back to Aurora, and he had yet to reach Nexon, where he hoped to start college. This rescue mission was an important matter of pride to him, since Derec and Ariel and the robot medical team had saved his life. Then Derec and Ariel had sent him away when each of them would have liked to use that ship personally.

He sighed and watched the screen. He expected most of the problem to be in locating them. The *Minneapolis* was outfitted to take them all back to Aurora together.

"PYRAMID LOCATED," said the computer. "CLOSE-UP ON SCREEN. PLEASE IDENTIFY."

On the viewscreen, the Compass Tower shone in the sunlight. The angle was from above, of course, and a little to one side. At this distance, it looked like a flawless model on a design display.

"That's it," said Jeff excitedly, sitting forward to look. "Can you land near it somewhere without smashing up anything?"

"SCANNING FOR A LOW-RISK LANDING SITE IN THE AREA," said the computer. "TO AVOID ALL CHANCE OF DAMAGE TO MANUFACTURED AND CONSTRUCTED PROPERTY, THIS CRAFT REQUIRES MORE LANDING SPACE THAN THE AREA HAS SO FAR OFFERED."

"Show me the area as you scan it," said Jeff. "Just try to land as close as you can."

"DISPLAYING."

Jeff watched the screen closely as the view pulled back to a greater height and began to move quickly across the landscape. At first he tried to recognize other places, such as a city plaza he remembered and the distinctive bronze dome of the Key Center. He couldn't find them. Then, as the camera continued to scan, he realized that they were covering a lot of area very quickly.

"Look for an open grassy region," he said. "It was just outside the city. I'm sure it wasn't more than a few kilometers from that tower."

"PERIMETER OF URBAN DEVELOPMENT NOT LO-CATED. SCANNING CONTINUES."

He watched as block after block of city passed beneath them. The robots had continued building, much faster than he had ever imagined. He couldn't afford to land on the other side of the planet. Derec and Ariel had lived close to the tower.

"Listen," he said. "Most of this population is robots. If they're damaged, they can be repaired. Just don't hit the buildings, 'cause we won't survive, either." He grinned at his own humor.

"CLARIFY."

"We have to land around here somewhere. Try to avoid the robots, but give us priority. Watch out for humans; other than that, find a place in the city near that tower where we can land. A park, a plaza, a big intersection. Something like that."

"SCANNING MODIFIED FOR MODERATE-RISK LANDING SITE. SITE SELECTED."

"Good," said Jeff. "That was quick. See if you can reach the city's central computer. Give it fair warning of our landing site so it can tell everybody to get out of the way."

"LINK ESTABLISHED. WARNING SENT AND AC-KNOWLEDGED. CURRENT SPEED REQUIRES WIDE TURN. PREPARE FOR LANDING IN APPROXIMATELY TWELVE MINUTES."

Jeff grinned. "Good job."

Eleven and a half minutes later, Jeff stared in tense fascination at the screen as the small ship sliced through the atmosphere at a low angle and came shooting straight toward the skyline. The *Minneapolis* was versatile enough to act as both a shuttle and starship, which was why he had chosen it. He trusted the computer, which would not allow him to come to harm if it could help it, despite being non-positronic . . . and yet even the computer couldn't prevent every malfunction. After all, he had just barely survived one crash here.

He was gripping the sides of the chair and sweating freely as the screen showed a broad boulevard stretching straight ahead. The ship was going to land along the pavement—did this thing have wheels? In a panic, he couldn't remember.

It must have; the computer wasn't stupid.

The streetfronts of a thousand buildings shot by in a blur, first below and then on both sides. The ship touched down and streaked along the empty street, suddenly decelerating sharply.

Everyone was out of the way; the city's central computer had done its part. The boulevard was as flat and straight as only a city of robots would construct. The ship came to a halt.

CHAPTER 9
WELCOME BACK

Jeff lay back in the chair panting heavily, with sweat running down his face and arms. That was a lot more frightening than he had expected . . . but a lot better than last time. The ship computer had been flawless.

Next time, he'd shut off that stupid viewscreen. Who needed to see that, anyhow?

"LANDING COMPLETED," said the computer cheerfully.

"Shut up," Jeff muttered.

He didn't want to stay in this can. Shakily, he got up and moved to the door. "Exit access," he instructed.

The door unlatched and opened. A flexible ladder extended from it. Jeff held the sides of the ladder firmly, turned, and climbed down.

On the street, he drew in a deep breath and looked around. It was Robot City, all right; it had the slidewalks, the tunnel stops, the clean, organized buildings and streets. On the other hand, it was totally unfamiliar.

A couple of humanoid robots were just now coming into view ahead. The central computer would have removed the alert, of course. He turned and looked behind him. A few more robots appeared, riding the slidewalks along the side of the boulevard.

The nearest robot approaching him was remarkably tall and full-chested.

"Excuse me," said Jeff. "I'm in need of assistance."

The Hunter robot took him firmly by the upper arm.

"Hey! Wait a minute. What are you doing?" He pulled back, but the robot didn't let go.

"I am detaining you," said the Hunter. "You are in custody and will remain so at least until you have been positively identified." It turned and began to walk.

"I'm Jeff Leong. That's no mystery." He hurried alongside, walking awkwardly, almost sideways.

"I am programmed to locate and detain two humans among the four intruders known to be in Robot City. You will not be harmed. However, you must come with me."

"And if I don't?" He demanded, looking up at the robot's expressionless face.

"You will come willingly or unwillingly. You will not be harmed. I prefer that you not resist."

The robot continued walking, dragging Jeff along with it. They stepped onto a slidewalk and went on walking.

"Who are you looking for?"

"The two humans named Derec and Ariel," said the Hunter. "Also an alien robot named Mandelbrot and a small living creature of undetermined type."

"Hold it. You think I'm Derec? Is that it?" Jeff tried to pull back again, to no avail.

"I am instructed to take you into custody pending identification," said the Hunter impassively.

"It's not necessary." Jeff managed to turn enough so he could walk straight ahead, at least. "Look, other robots know me. Contact the medical team. What was their name? Some kind of hospital. A Human Medical Center, or something like that. They can tell you who I am. Call them through the central computer."

The robot did not respond.

"Are you calling them?"

It still did not respond.

"Not programmed for that, I suppose," said Jeff. He sighed. "Welcome back to Robot City, Jeff."

They walked along the moving slidewalk for quite some time. Jeff's belongings were still stashed in the ship, of course; he had intended to grab his personal luggage after getting directions to Derec and Ariel. Resigned to a long and probably frustrating interrogation by more robots, he marched along in step.

A certain amount of foot traffic and vehicular traffic went by, but Jeff was sure that it was less than he remembered from his previous visit. Somewhat belatedly, he was recalling just how many unexplained oddities this city had had. Then, lost in thought, he was not paying particular attention to the details around him until he heard a screech of tires coming up right behind him.

Jeff flinched and whirled around. The Hunter holding him turned its head but did not break stride.

A humanoid robot was just leaping out of the cab of a large, halted vehicle.

"Mandelbrot!" Jeff shouted. "Tell this robot who I am, will you? It thinks—"

He was interrupted as the Hunter spun completely around, at the same time yanking him to the side away from Mandelbrot. The robot's hold on him did not loosen even for a moment.

"You are harming the human," said Mandelbrot to the Hunter, in a remarkably unemotional voice. He stepped onto the slidewalk and approached them.

"I am not harming him." The Hunter's voice was equally calm. It stood still.

Jeff understood that Mandelbrot had spoken aloud so that he could hear. Apparently Mandelbrot intended to rescue him— and that implied changes here in the city that were completely beyond Jeff's expectations.

Jeff let out as loud and intense a scream as he could and dropped to his knees on the slidewalk, which was still moving.

The Hunter still had him by the arm.

"Release him!" Mandelbrot shouted, striding forward and lifting Jeff in his own arms. "Hunter, you are inefficient! You are violating the First Law!"

"You . . . are . . . Mandelbrot . . . the fugitive robot," the Hunter said slowly. It was quivering slightly, its functioning impaired by the uncertainty that it might have harmed Jeff. Yet it had not let go.

Mandelbrot gripped the wrist of the Hunter and gently held Jeff's captive arm, as well. "Release him," he ordered again. "I will take him into custody."

"You . . . are . . . not . . . fooling me," said the Hunter. "Step . . . away."

Jeff could see that. The Hunter knew that Mandelbrot himself was a fugitive from the central computer, so his words were all suspect. However, the combination of his accusation and Jeff's play-acting was enough to raise a reasonable doubt in its mind, and the force of the First Law was so great that it was now hesitant to act.

"Mandelbrot, carry me," he pleaded, in as anxious a voice as he could muster. "He's hurt me."

The Hunter was in trouble, but not fully convinced. Mandelbrot did manage to force its grip open, however, and remove Jeff's arm. Then he picked up Jeff around the waist, jumped off the slidewalk onto the stationary shoulder, and ran for his truck.

"Stop!" The Hunter moved to action the moment Jeff was free, though it was still not at full capacity.

Jeff was facing backward as Mandelbrot ran with him, and could see the Hunter gradually entering a slow run after them. The Hunter's instructions were still in effect.

"It's already sent out a call for other Hunters," said Mandelbrot, still running. "You will get an explanation at a safer time. For now, when I hoist you into the back of this vehicle, lie down and hang on. You will be safest that way."

"Uh—okay—" Jeff complied as Mandelbrot jumped into the cab and drove off fast.

Derec was awakened from a deep sleep by the sound of the big door opening. Light hit his closed eyelids and he reluctantly opened them with a squint. So Mandelbrot was back. He took in a deep breath, hoping to wake up completely and find food being offered.

The vehicle entered the building and then Ariel was already closing the door again.

Mandelbrot turned in the cab and helped another figure in the back to his feet.

"Say!" Ariel cried excitedly. "Is that . . . that's Jeff!"

Amazed, Derec forced himself up on one elbow. His back and shoulders ached painfully.

"Hi, gang," said Jeff. He stood looking around at them all

from the back of the truck. Then Mandelbrot lifted him down.

"Jeff," said Derec. He grimaced as he sat up all the way. "What the . . . what are you doing here?"

He gave an embarrassed shrug. "I came to get you. To rescue you from Robot City."

Derec felt his jaw drop open.

Ariel clapped both hands over her mouth.

"Ooooo," said Wolruf.

"Oh, no." Derec rubbed his forehead, stifling an embarrassed smile of his own.

"What is it?" Jeff asked, looking at them all one after another. "What's wrong? Don't you want to leave any more?"

"Jeff." Ariel went over to him and gave him a hug. "You actually came back for us. That's wonderful. Please don't misunderstand. It really means a great deal. Thank you."

Jeff hugged her back lightly, clearly uncomfortable. "I don't get it. What's going on?"

"Jeff," said Derec. "We can get off the planet now if we want. In fact, we can travel pretty far—as far as Earth and back. We . . . I . . . have a different problem now."

"You can travel now?"

"I'm afraid so," said Derec.

Jeff looked at Ariel, who shrugged. Then he gave a short laugh, shaking his head. "Mind if I sit down?" He collapsed on the floor where he was, not too far from Derec.

"I thought you were going to send someone else back," said Derec. "I had no idea you'd come yourself."

"How did you find it?" Mandelbrot asked. "If you remember, I had no navigational data to give you."

"I had a computer cross-reference the Aurora–Nexus route with what little I knew. It worked." Jeff ran a hand through his black hair, staring at the floor. "I'm a little shocked. But I'm glad you haven't been stranded."

"How *did* you get here?" Derec asked.

"I was picked up by a ship headed back to Aurora. Once I got back there, I put together the location where I was picked up, the length of time it took me to get there, and the nearest stars. A computer gave me the likely directions, but I had to try several before I got the right one." He shrugged. "The hard part was getting my father to spring for the rental of a ship. And now I have to tell him it was unnecessary."

"Well. . . ." Ariel started.

Jeff turned to look at her.

"We could still use some help," she said. "We have to find Dr. Avery before his robots get ahold of us."

"Avery! Did you say Dr. Avery?" Jeff sat up straight.

"You've heard of him?" Ariel said, dropping down to sit next to him. "Where?"

"Mandelbrot, Wolruf," said Derec. "Come closer and follow this. It may turn out to be important."

"Well," said Jeff. "I tried to explain to my father what I needed the ship for and he reminded me that this weird guy named Avery once had some wild plans about a planet with a planned community sort of like this one."

"Wait a minute! This was supposed to be a secret," said Ariel. "My mother funded it. How does your father know about it?"

"He doesn't, really. It's just that Dr. Avery gave away some hints when we met him."

"Met him?" Derec and Ariel cried in unison.

"Look, I don't remember it very well—"

"We've all had a few memory problems," Ariel said with annoyance. "Come on, this is important to us."

"When?" Derec demanded. "Recently? Back on Aurora?"

"No, no, no. A long time ago. A couple of years ago."

Derec settled back. "What happened?"

"He was still planning then, I bet," said Ariel. "Considering how fast these robots work, that's plenty of time."

"He came to consult with my father," said Jeff. "My father is a professor of Spacer cultural studies. His specialty is tracing the development and evolution of the various Spacer communities."

"What does that mean?" Derec asked.

"They're comparative studies," said Jeff. "What planets have in common and what they don't. How they're organized. How their values differ. Stuff like that."

"Your father must be an expert in that, huh?" Ariel said. "That's why Avery sought him out."

"I guess." Jeff shrugged. "Anyhow, a couple of years ago, this Dr. Avery asked to consult informally with him. My father was real impressed with the guy. He said Avery was an eccentric genius, and made me tag along to meet him."

"What did he want to talk about?" Derec asked.

"He was asking about social matrices," said Jeff. "In particular, how my father would set up a utopia, if he could."

"Utopia." Derec exchanged a glance with Ariel. "That's how he viewed this experiment, isn't it?"

She nodded. "Jeff. We can use any clues you have to Avery's personality."

"I can tell you what I remember. Why do you have to find him, anyway?"

"He implanted a kind of . . . well, sort of a disease in Derec that only he can remove. We have to figure out where he is on the planet. Can you tell us what he's like?"

"I hate to tell you this, but I don't remember him very well." Jeff looked at all of them apologetically. "I wasn't that old, and I didn't really care about seeing him. I went because my father wanted me to meet this genius. He said it would be a good experience for me. The truth is, I didn't get much out of it."

"Anything," said Ariel. "Just start talking. Maybe things will come back to you."

"Well . . . my father had a very high regard for him. More than usual. I mean, he's surrounded by very capable people all the time. They were pretty friendly for a while."

"Then what?" Derec asked. "Dr. Avery left Aurora, I suppose?"

Jeff shook his head. "Not right away. That is, he came and went for a time. My father had some sort of falling out with him, I think, but I never bothered to ask about it."

"Are you sure you don't know why they stopped being friends?" Ariel asked. "It might turn out to be important."

"I think he was pretty egotistical. I got that impression right away. And he was definitely eccentric. I guess my father just got tired of listening to him."

"That fits my mother's description," Ariel said to Derec. "Can we use that somehow?"

"I don't know. We've all found dealing with him unpleasant." Derec shrugged. "Mandelbrot, you can correlate data the best of us all. What do you think?"

"We have information about Robot City," said Mandelbrot. "And we have information about Dr. Avery. However, we don't have the necessary correlations to narrow the scope of his whereabouts."

"What about our staying here?" Derec asked. "Are we safer staying here longer, or should we move?"

"I only have a guess," said the robot. "I again used an evasive route in returning here, but the fact that the truck vanished from sight in the same general area as last time will narrow the Hunters' scope considerably. On the other hand, traveling somewhere else clearly provides more data to the central computer of our whereabouts every time we are witnessed by any robot in the city."

Derec sighed and rubbed the stiff muscles in his legs. "Thank you for the lecture. What's your conclusion?"

"We are better off remaining here for the remainder of the day. At nightfall, travel will be safer than staying here. These are both calculated risks, not cert—"

"I understand," said Derec. He gritted his teeth and lay down again. Normally he wanted to know how Mandelbrot formed his judgements because the robot's consistent logic could be informative. Now he was just too tired and in too much pain for that.

"Maybe we should all rest," said Ariel. "If we're going to go somewhere else after dark."

"Good idea," said Wolruf.

Derec closed his eyes. He heard Wolruf pad away, presumably to relax in a spot of her choosing.

"I was planning to go out again to seek a food source," said Mandelbrot, "but I now consider it too risky. All of you can remain healthy through the day without sustenance. When we travel at night, we may find food in some way. Is this acceptable?"

"Sure," Derec muttered, without opening his eyes.

"All right," said Ariel.

"You know," Jeff said slowly, "I have plenty of supplies on board the *Minneapolis*. I didn't realize food was a problem for you. The only question is how to get it."

"I doubt it's a simple question," said Ariel. "It must be well guarded by now."

They could have dismantled it by now, Derec thought, but he was too exhausted to speak up.

"Perhaps we can look into this," said Mandelbrot. "Though the risk is very high."

"How about a review of the whole situation?" Jeff asked. "I never did know the origin of this place. Would you mind giving me the entire story? We apparently have the rest of the day."

"You know, Jeff," said Ariel, "you really don't have to get mixed up in this. If we can get you back on board your ship, you can get out of here again."

"I'm ready to help."

"I don't think we can ask you to do that." She lowered her voice. "You haven't heard what Dr. Avery has done to Derec."

"I'm staying," Jeff said firmly. "I came here to repay a debt. Since you don't need help getting off the planet anymore, I'll repay it with help you do need."

"Maybe you should know what you're getting involved in before you decide."

"Go ahead," said Jeff. "But I'm staying, period."

Derec drifted off to sleep to the sound of Ariel's voice recounting their story.

He awoke again, much later, as strong arms slid under him and lifted him. "What's happening?" His throat was rough and dry. He cleared it, opening his eyes.

Mandelbrot was carrying him to the back of the truck.

"Time to go, huh?" Derec smiled weakly as he settled onto the truck bed.

"We're all here," said Ariel, next to him. "Mandelbrot's in charge so far. Ready?"

"Sure. Where are we going?"

"We're going after my supplies," said Jeff.

"What?" Derec struggled to sit up, looking at them in surprise. "That's a perfect trap. What's the plan?"

"We don't have one yet," said Ariel. "Mandelbrot couldn't get any information about the ship through the central computer without giving himself away, so we don't know what kind of security it has around it or anything."

"I don't like this at all," said Derec. He turned to Mandelbrot, who was pushing the button on the wall to open the door. "Mandelbrot, this sounds like walking into a trap to me. Have you considered that?"

"Yes." Mandelbrot hurried back to the cab of the truck as the door began to open into a Robot City twilight.

"You have? Then why are we doing this?"

"The plan is flexible. All I intend to do now is take an evasive route back to the landing site for observation. We will not take unnecessary risks."

"Well . . . okay." Derec sat back against the wall of the truck. If he could just feel better, he could be more persuasive. Or help make plans. It was just so hard to concentrate.

The truck rolled out onto the empty street. The robot population seemed to be getting thinner all the time. That was good for his purposes, Derec thought, but the mysteries remained. What was the purpose of the robot assembly points . . . and where was Dr. Avery?

Robot City had street lights, but they were not as bright or as frequent as in other cities. The robots' superior vision made more light unnecessary. The entire planet was a city of technological marvels and striking robotic capabilities.

"What did Avery get from your father?" Derec asked suddenly. "He's called Professor Leong? What have we seen in this city that Professor Leong provided?"

"I haven't seen anything like that," said Jeff. "He was talking about culture. I've seen science, technology, and architecture taken to new heights, but that's all."

"The play," said Ariel. "We had the robots do *Hamlet* here after you left. That is, Derec chose it but the robots were ready for it. Some of them were involved with robot creativity."

"The arts," said Derec. "Of course. And maybe a system of ethics beyond the Laws of Robotics—"

"The Laws of Humanics they used to talk about," Ariel said excitedly. "Some of this crazy stuff is starting to make sense now."

"Instead of being just oddities." Derec nodded. "Robots are too logical to leave a lot of loose ends."

"Rrobot creativity," said Wolruf. "Came at ssame time Dr. Averry returrned to Robot City."

"That's right," said Ariel. "And now, after he's apparently reprogrammed all the robots, there's no sign of it."

"The creative impulse caused too much trouble," said Derec. "But originally, he programmed some artistic abilities into his robots. Jeff, does this fit what you remember?"

"That's along the right line, yeah. And I remember now that he had one interest in particular."

"Really? What was it?"

"Cultures that could endure."

"Endure," said Derec. "You mean like republics and empires

and so on? Dynasties and stuff like that?"

Jeff shook his head in the darkening light as the truck slowed for an intersection, then speeded up again. "Cultures. They generally outlast politics. They evolve in response to politics and economics and technology, but they have lives of their own. My father called them the sum of all the disciplines."

The truck came to a halt, drawing their attention. Derec looked out and saw that they had stopped on an overpass. The bright twinkling lights of Robot City stretched in all directions, implying the shapes of buildings and streets by their patterns in swooping curves and mighty blocks and spiraling towers and a fully reliable grid on the ground.

"Down there," said Jeff. "That's the boulevard I landed on, running parallel with this one. See between those buildings there?"

"I see it," said Ariel. "Just barely."

"I dare not take the truck any closer," said Mandelbrot, standing in the open cab to face them. "I can approach it on foot and survey the security measures."

"Hold it," said Derec. "If they left it just sitting there, it has to be a trap. Mandelbrot, that means they're ready for you, too, in some way. They wouldn't leave bait like that just waiting to be flown away."

"Too bad we can't move it," said Jeff.

"Wait a minute," said Ariel. "Maybe Mandelbrot can communicate with its computer."

"I doubt they left the ship operational," said Derec. "That doesn't make sense, either."

"Unless they're overconfident of their security measures," said Jeff. "Mandelbrot, if you want to try, it's a ten-passenger Hayashi-Smith named *Minneapolis*. It's non-positronic but it's smart enough to handle the flight instructions I give it, which are pretty general. That's about all I know about it."

"I am currently trying standard frequencies," said Mandelbrot. "The customary range is small. No response."

"Good," said Derec.

"*What?*" Ariel demanded.

"Maybe we have a chance after all."

"What do you mean?" Jeff asked.

"If we're lucky, the only way they disabled the ship was to

disconnect the computer. Mandelbrot, your comlink can send out the same impulses it did."

"I might be able to start the ship," said Mandelbrot, "but I can't fly it from here. The boulevard is too narrow and I'm not familiar with the ship itself."

"I can't 'elp 'u, eitherr," said Wolruf apologetically. "Can navigate, but giving orrders to Mandelbrot takess too long for shuttle takeoff. And 'ave no line of sight from herr, eitherr."

"We don't have to fly it," said Derec. "The boulevard goes straight. All we have to do is get it away from their security long enough to get inside and grab the supplies."

"The robots would know that," said Jeff. "Don't you think they must have accounted for that somehow?"

"Maybe," said Derec. "But remember how logical this place is. The Hunters don't have much experience with devious thinking."

"They were programmed by a paranoid," Ariel pointed out.

"It's worth a shot," said Derec.

"I believe I can make it go straight," said Mandelbrot. "I suggest, however, that we first take the truck to the rendezvous site so that we are waiting when it arrives. It will not take the Hunters long to catch up with it."

Derec's heart was pounding with excitement, and the adrenaline seemed to be loosening up his muscles. He grinned. "Let's go!"

Mandelbrot drove the truck a much longer time than Derec had expected, but the distance he covered made sense. The fifteen kilometers the ship would travel down the boulevard to reach them was virtually nothing to it, even in its shuttle mode. Mandelbrot pulled the truck into a side street and brought it close to the intersection with the boulevard. Then he stopped the truck and sat motionless.

"I guess he's concentrating," said Ariel.

"They ought to rename this street Minneapolis Boulevard," said Jeff, grinning. "If this works, anyhow."

Derec was tingling with excitement. "Wolruf, when you and Mandelbrot are both inside, you can fly this thing, right?"

"Rright." A slash of street light cut across her face as she gave a nod and a caninoid grin.

"Here it comes," said Jeff.

A high, even whine was coming toward them in the distance, growing louder as Derec listened. They sat motionless, unable to see around the corner of the nearest building. Only Mandelbrot was visible, and Derec watched his dark, motionless profile as the sound grew louder.

Soon the sound was almost deafening. The ship pulled into view in the intersection, seeming to loom over them in the garish light and deep shadows, both huge and wonderful. Then it stopped.

Mandelbrot stood up and turned to help Derec out of the truck. The others took it as a signal to climb out themselves and run for the waiting ship.

Mandelbrot picked up Derec under one arm to save time by carrying him. At the robot's command, the door opened ahead of them and the ladder slid to the ground. Derec looked down the boulevard as Mandelbrot ran with him.

A crowd of robots was rushing toward them in the far distance. Hunters were running along the moving slidewalks. Function robots of various sizes and shapes were rolling and driving down the boulevard. They constituted the surprise element of the trap, now neutralized by the stealing of the bait.

The function robots did not have positronic brains to think with, but they could follow orders from the Hunters to move in paths that would block or even ram the ship and the truck. The fastest of them were coming on rapidly.

Mandelbrot set Derec down on the highest rung of the ladder that he could reach. Derec's foot slipped on the ladder. As he clung to the ladder with another nervous glance at the oncoming rush, he felt Mandelbrot take him under his arms and lift him. Mandelbrot climbed the ladder, holding Derec up until he could deposit him inside the ship. Jeff and Ariel pulled him to one side as the robot entered last.

Wolruf was already in the navigator's seat looking at the override controls. The ladder retracted and the door closed as Mandelbrot took the pilot's seat.

"Straight on down boulevarrd," said Wolruf. "Space is enough forr takeoff."

Mandelbrot was reaching for the manual controls. "These will be safer than risking comlink control. Everyone, please strap in."

"We're all strapped into seats," said Jeff. "I'm sure glad you can do this. All I can do is tell the computer what I want."

Just as the ship began to move forward, a heavy thump struck the rear of the ship. The impact was faint but clearly noticeable.

"Damage insignificant," said Wolruf.

The ship was picking up speed. Another crash against the rear of the ship swayed it crookedly for a moment before Mandelbrot brought it back into line. A horrible screeching sound raked along the left side.

"They can't do much," said Derec. "The First Law won't let the Hunters order anything that might cause a crash. They must know by now they can't stop the ship without knocking us out of control."

"Hope you're right," Jeff said grimly, as another thump shook the rear of the ship.

That was the last one, however. The ship had left the last of the function robots behind and was angling steeply into the air.

"I have chosen to go into a low orbit," said Mandelbrot. "This ship does not carry large amounts of fuel for shuttle mode and it will be needed for landing here and also for Jeff's eventual trip away from the planet. However, as long as we are off the surface of the planet, we are safe from the robots of Robot City."

"That's a relief," said Derec. "Unless they've developed a space program we don't know about."

"The navigational sensorrs indicate no ssign of that," said Wolruf. "Suggesst I take manual controls. Mandelbrot can reconnect ship computerr."

"Agreed," said Mandelbrot.

"The First Law won't let them shoot us down or anything like that," said Ariel. "But they can monitor us, can't they? And have a welcoming committee anywhere we land?"

Mandelbrot now had a panel open by the controls and was studying the interior. "This craft is small and its shuttle mode offers high maneuverability. We should be able to land with an evasive pattern that will make our site unpredictable until the last few seconds."

"I'm glad to hear it," said Jeff. "This planet is never dull, is it?"

"No," said Derec, "but it hasn't always been this dangerous, either. One time we had to solve a human murder, and another time we had to solve the apparent murder of a robot. But it's only recently that we've been anyone's target."

Jeff laughed. "Last time I was here, they took my brain out of my head and stuck it in a robot. That struck *me* as dangerous."

Ariel laughed. Derec grinned in spite of the pain in his ribs when he started to laugh. Even Wolruf glanced back over her shoulder with an amused look.

"I'm glad you're okay," said Ariel. "And thanks again for coming back, even if it was under mistaken assumptions."

Derec felt a twinge of jealousy but said nothing. Now that the crisis was over, his body was stiffening up rapidly again. He reclined in his seat and felt the adhesions snapping in his back.

"I believe this connection is now sufficient," said Mandelbrot. "Jeff, will you test the VoiceCommand?"

"Hayashi-Smith *Minneapolis* ship computer," said Jeff. "Please acknowledge."

"STANDING BY," said the computer.

"Can you assume flight duties?"

"AFFIRMATIVE."

"Do so, maintaining status quo."

"FLIGHT DUTY ASSUMED."

"Also record the following voices into your VoiceCommand and prepare to follow any of them." Jeff nodded to the others.

Each of them spoke in turn to the computer.

"What's our next move?" Derec asked. "We're safe for the moment, but we aren't any closer to Dr. Avery, are we?"

"We know a little more about his aims for Robot City," said Ariel. "Based on Professor Leong's knowledge of him."

"But we haven't turned that into a clue to his location," said Derec. "Mandelbrot, any ideas?"

"One, Derec," said the robot. "Computer. Scan for any sign of large-scale crop growth or organic chemical stores."

"SCANNING," said the computer.

"Dr. Avery's food source may not be in a quantity or storage facility that we can locate from here," said Mandelbrot, with a humanlike shrug. "It is only a possibility."

"Are carbon compounds used for anything else here?" Jeff asked, looking around at everyone. "Besides that hospital place I was in, or whatever you called it."

"I'm not sure," said Derec.

"We are safe in saying that the amounts are quite small,"

said Mandelbrot. "In addition, the amount of food required for a single human is small, as well. Our best hope of finding a source in quantity is the chance that Dr. Avery may wish to extend his interest in culture to the art of cuisine."

"Or at least, maybe he wants better food than those chemical processors give you," said Ariel. "Fresh produce, maybe."

"Hey! Speaking of which," said Jeff, "what did we grab this ship for in the first place? Come on, let's eat. Ariel, the compartment's next to you."

Jeff distributed rations to everyone but Mandelbrot, even locating some items Wolruf could tolerate.

"EXTENSIVE AGRICULTURAL GROWTH LOCATED," said the computer. "COMING ON SCREEN."

"Close-up," ordered Mandelbrot. "Identify if possible."

Everyone watched the screen. A tiny dark spot rapidly grew into a green rectangle. That rectangle, a moment later, was clearly a quilt of many different shades of green. On extreme close-up, the shapes of the plants came clear.

"MANY CROPS ARE PRESENT. THEY INCLUDE CORN, SORGHUM, WHEAT, AND BEETS. AT FIRST SCAN, AURORAN STRAINS OF EARTH-NATIVE PLANTS PREDOMINATE. MANY CROPS ARE UNIDENTIFIABLE AT THIS HEIGHT AND ANGLE."

"Maybe the robots bred some of them themselves," said Ariel. "Or they're native here."

"Pull back the view," said Mandelbrot. "Show the surrounding geography."

The view drew back to show the spine of a mountain range. It was geologically old, exhibiting the gentle edges and curves of long erosion. The range was fully forested but occasionally dotted with buildings. The agricultural park was nestled in a high-altitude valley within the mountain range itself.

"It's not city," said Jeff. "It's the first place I've seen since coming back that isn't all built up."

"Us, too," said Ariel.

"The robots are probably using the forests for lumber and the slopes for industrial power or something," said Derec. "They don't generally let anything go to waste. But those crops are all food. I think this is it. Mandelbrot?"

"The probability is extremely high that this is a human food source. We must investigate it. I remind everyone that Dr. Avery himself is not necessarily present."

"It's a start," said Jeff. "Now what?"

"First we must find a place to land," said Mandelbrot. "These mountains are unsuitable. Second, I suggest that Wolruf and I scout the location alone. Third, the safest place for the rest of you to wait is in the air."

"Makes sense to me," said Jeff. "You can use your comlink to reach us when necessary, and we can fly this thing ourselves again now."

"Derec?" Ariel asked.

"Yeah, okay." He shifted uncomfortably, angry that he couldn't participate more. Still, this plan was simple enough.

"Computer," said Mandelbrot. "Scan for landing sites as close to the crop field as possible."

"CURRENTLY OUT OF VISUAL RANGE," said the computer. "SCANNING WILL BEGIN WITH THE NEXT ORBITAL PASS."

"We'll need multiple sites," said Mandelbrot. "The Hunters will undoubtedly secure the first one after we've used it."

"Computer," said Derec, with effort. "Don't allow our orbital route to give away our interest in that area."

"ACKNOWLEDGED."

Derec collapsed again. He wasn't sleepy, but he was worn out. The short period of excitement had revitalized him, but now he was paying the price.

Everyone seemed to be unwinding from their escape in the ship. Derec lay with his eyes closed and he heard someone switch out the light directly over him. The darkness on his lids was a relief.

No one spoke for some time. Then, quietly, he heard the computer again.

"NEAREST LANDING SITES TO AGRICULTURAL PARK COMING ON SCREEN AS FOLLOWS: FIVE WITHIN FIVE-KILOMETER RADIUS; TWO MORE WITHIN TEN KILOMETERS; THREE MORE WITHIN TWENTY KILOMETERS."

"Are any of them in relatively uninhabited areas? Especially away from urban streets?" Mandelbrot asked.

"DISPLAYING THE FIVE CLOSEST SITES. THESE ARE

THE ONLY SITES NOT USING CITY PAVEMENT."

Derec forced his eyes open. He hated feeling left out.

"It's an ocean," said Jeff, in surprise.

"A stretch of beach," said Ariel.

As they watched, five separate areas of beach on the screen were colored lightly by the computer.

"THESE SITES REPRESENT STRETCHES OF SAND LONG ENOUGH AND FIRM ENOUGH FOR A SAFE LANDING," said the computer.

"For the purpose of evading the Hunters, this might as well be one landing site," said Mandelbrot. "When they see the first, they will find the others."

"We'll have to take the chance," said Derec. "We'll drop off you and Wolruf as fast as we can and take off again. Then we'll go back into orbit until we hear from you."

"Or until your fuel level reaches minimum," said Mandelbrot. "I will alert the computer to warn you when you must land."

Derec closed his eyes again.

"All right," said Jeff.

"Computer," said Mandelbrot. "On the next orbit, take an evasive route down to the first of the landing sites. Avoid revealing our destination as long as you can."

"ACKNOWLEDGED."

Most of the next orbit was uneventful, but Derec found the evasive maneuvers extremely unpleasant. The ship descended, turned as sharply as it could, ascended again, turned again. Each change shifted his weight and pressed his aching muscles. None of the others seemed to notice.

The changes began to include speed as the ship worked its crooked way down toward the planet. Derec gripped the strap holding him in both hands and clenched his teeth against the pain shooting through his back. Finally the descent smoothed out and he realized they were about to land.

The ship landed on a surface that listed somewhat to the left and halted so suddenly that everyone was thrown forward against their restraining straps. The door opened automatically and the ladder extended. Mandelbrot and Wolruf were ready to go. Moments later, the door closed again and the ship waited briefly for them to get a safe distance from the ship.

"PREPARED FOR LIFT-OFF AS ORDERED," said the computer. "PLEASE INSTRUCT."

"Return to the same altitude we just left," said Jeff. "Uh, use evasive pattern and take a different orbit when we get there."

"ACKNOWLEDGED."

The acceleration pressed Derec back against his seat again. He closed his eyes, resigned to the ride, and lay still.

CHAPTER 12

DESERTED STREETS

Mandelbrot and Wolruf ran straight up the beach. The sand was pale blue and packed hard all the way to the line where the ground cover began. There they climbed up the dip between two high, rounded, grassy dunes.

"Careful," said Mandelbrot. "The Hunters will be on their way here already."

Wolruf nodded.

They moved cautiously over the next rise and Mandelbrot found the edge of the urban area. The dunes were bordered by a curving boulevard. Ahead of them, a smaller street stretched away from them, lined with buildings on both sides.

"No one is 'err," said Wolruf.

The streets were deserted in all directions.

"We will be very easy to spot here," said Mandelbrot. "I have no crowd to get lost in and you are now on the Hunters' list."

"Should move."

Mandelbrot looked toward the mountains that loomed over them slightly to the left. "The valley itself is no farther than five kilometers, but the mountains begin much closer. The greatest danger to us is crossing the city to reach them."

"Greatest danger to us iss waiting 'err," said Wolruf.

"Agreed. Let's go." Mandelbrot started across the boulevard, striding at a pace that was fast but dignified.

No robots were visible in either direction. On the first city block, they stayed near the edges of the buildings themselves and glanced inside any doorways or windows that offered a view. The city was functioning here without humanoid robots.

"Assembly points," said Wolruf. "Robots 'err have already lefft." She glanced behind them, over her shoulder. "'Unterss could come from any direction."

"A tunnel stop would help us considerably," said Mandelbrot. "If we stay on this street we will encounter one, if they were built with the same frequency in this area as in the area we are familiar with." He paused to look inside a window. Inside, function robots were scuttling about on their duties.

"Maybe they didn't build any 'err at all," said Wolruf as she trotted alongside to keep up.

"That is possible. If this portion of the city is built on sand, then tunneling is more difficult. However, these robots do not seem to factor difficulty into their considerations."

"Therr," Wolruf said emphatically, pointing ahead.

A humanoid robot was just disappearing from sight around a corner ahead of them.

Mandelbrot reached down to lift Wolruf, and began to run— not at full speed, but quickly enough to make up some ground.

"Careful," said Wolruf, clutching him around the neck.

"I believe that a Hunter this close to us would have come in this direction," said Mandelbrot. "However, I do not want to contact any robot without the chance to observe the situation first. Pursuit is the only recourse."

A moment later, they turned the corner after the other robot. He was now riding a slidewalk, standing still as it carried him parallel to the mountain range. Mandelbrot hurried to the slidewalk and then walked slowly after him once they were on it.

"I think I understand," he said quietly. "Either this humanoid cannot be replaced here by function robots, or else he is one of the last, possibly the very last, in this area to follow his migration programming."

"If that iss the case, we should forget about 'im," said Wolruf. "Go to the mountains and 'ide from 'unters. Find Avery."

"We will be safer taking evasive action than simply racing the Hunters to the mountains. In fact, we should avoid indicating to them what our destination is, if possible. I am hoping to find a group of humanoid robots to observe so that we can imitate their actions without being witnessed by them."

"Too late," said Wolruf, looking back over his shoulder. "'Err come 'unters."

Mandelbrot turned to look. One humanoid, clearly a Hunter by his size and sensors, was riding a distant slidewalk toward the landing site.

"Good. They intend to pick up our trail at the beach. That gives us a little more time." Mandelbrot set Wolruf on her feet. "I will try to manage among the robots. See if you can reach the agricultural park. I will attempt to meet you there."

Wolruf hissed a kind of agreement and hopped off the slidewalk. Then she darted away.

Mandelbrot considered a number of options for himself instantly and chose one. He sent a distress alert to the robot ahead of him through his comlink.

"I am in need of assistance," he said.

The other robot turned to face him, then stepped onto the stationary shoulder to wait for Mandelbrot. "What is wrong?"

"I am on the verge of physically shutting down." That was true; Mandelbrot neglected to say that it was voluntary. "Please take me to the nearest repair facility. Report me as a malfunctioned robot, failure unknown."

"Agreed."

Mandelbrot froze in place but kept his positronic brain functioning. He had deliberately avoided identifying himself.

This robot was complying with Mandelbrot's request under a subtle but real compulsion. The Third Law of Robotics required robots to avoid harm to themselves through action or inaction but did not specifically require them to keep other robots from harm. However, in the robot society of Robot City, Mandelbrot had observed that such cooperation was common. Perhaps it was even programmed. In any case, he knew he could count on another robot's help, at least in the absence of more pressing problems.

The robot stepped back onto the slidewalk next to him. Apparently the nearest repair facility was in this direction. At least it would offer a kind of camouflage from the Hunters since he would not just be wandering around by himself or, worse, with a highly recognizable caninoid alien.

He hoped Wolruf could make it to the mountains. She was still of no interest to most robots, though they could act as witnesses to her presence and her direction for the Hunters. In the forested mountains she would have a better chance.

At present, the Hunters would almost certainly be tracking them by infrared heat sensors. When they had followed Mandelbrot and Wolruf to the point where they had mounted the slidewalk, they would ride it while scanning the shoulder for the spot or spots where their quarry had gotten off again. He rode on.

Finally the other robot lifted him and stepped off the slidewalk. This kept Mandelbrot's robot body heat off the ground; the Hunters would not be able to detect where he had left the slidewalk. However, they would be on Wolruf's trail without a problem.

Wolruf trotted down the empty sidewalk, alert on all sides for the sight, sound, or scent of humanoid robots. The city here was as striking as ever; she passed a gigantic, many-faceted dome glittering in the sunshine, a spiraling jade-green skyscraper that resembled loosely twisted ribbons frozen in midfall, and a multitude of combined pyramidal, hexagonal, and conical shapes. The quiet hum of machinery and the occasional function robots moving about told her that the city was still active here.

The absence of humanoids was eerie. The city was just too big and elaborate to seem normal with deserted streets and nearly vacant buildings. She felt exposed.

Wolruf grinned to herself as she turned corners, circled blocks, doubled back, and then moved on, always working her way closer to the mountains that were so invitingly close. As a navigator, she was no stranger to evasive maneuvers. She had not usually conducted them on foot, however, or been limited to one plane.

She was not certain how successful these maneuvers would be. If the Hunters possessed heat sensors that could consistently choose the warmest trail, then she was not going to confuse them by crisscrossing her path. Instead, she was just wasting time and letting them get closer. After she had done a little more of that, she resorted to a zigzag pattern that angled her toward the mountains more quickly.

When she reached the edge of the city, she stopped to consider her next move. A long boulevard lined the base of the first foothill; beyond it, the forest began. If she could disguise her point of entry into the mountains, it would help her a great deal.

She hopped onto the slidewalk that ran down the side of the boulevard, looking around. The Hunters could be right behind her or a long way back; she had no way of knowing without risking them seeing her. She could be sure, however, that they were coming with that inexorable robot logic and single-mindedness.

Nor could she ride here indefinitely; she could be seen easily by anyone looking down the straightaway. She jumped off again.

What she needed was a mobile function robot she could ride across the boulevard, or anything else that would keep moving after she left it, so that the traces of her body heat would be carried away. With an anxious glance behind her, she turned a corner and looked down the street.

It was empty.

Time was growing short. She would either have to find a way to break her trail, or else leave a track into the mountains that any Hunter could follow.

She started down the street, peering inside any windows she could reach.

"ORBIT ATTAINED," said the ship computer. "PLEASE INSTRUCT."

"Maintain altitude," said Jeff. "Vary the route at random."

"ACKNOWLEDGED."

Jeff turned to look at Derec. He was reclining in his seat, eyes closed, jaw clenched. Jeff unstrapped and moved over to him.

"What is it?" Ariel asked.

"These seats convert into berths. If you'll unstrap him, I'll get the seat all the way down flat. Then flexible privacy walls pull down from the ceiling."

"I see."

They worked in silence, watching Derec. He was clearly awake, but in no mood to converse. When he was lying down comfortably, Jeff pulled down the walls, leaving one open just enough for him to see out if he wished.

Jeff and Ariel sat down in the two control seats in the front.

"Can we do anything for him?" Jeff asked.

"No," Ariel whispered.

He looked at her in surprise.

Her eyes were wide and staring at the blank viewscreen on the console.

"Ariel? What's wrong?"

She didn't respond.

He took hold of her arm, gently, and moved his face in front of her unwavering gaze. "Ariel. Can you see me?"

Her eyes were steady, open, and beginning to water.

Jeff felt a tickle of fear along the back of his neck. Ariel had told him something of the chemfets in Derec and her memory loss and regrowth. However, he had had the impression that she was getting much better. Now he was alone in orbit with both of them and didn't know if he should try to help or what he could do.

"Computer," he said. "Review landing sites. Skip the ones on the beach. They'll be guarded."

"LANDING SITES COMING ON SCREEN."

"Which one is the closest to the crops now?"

"IT IS MARKED IN BLUE."

"Can you describe it?"

"IT IS A MAIN THOROUGHFARE IN THIS PART OF THE CITY, STRAIGHT AND OF SUFFICIENT SIZE FOR A SAFE LANDING. THE SHIP WILL HALT APPROXIMATELY 6.4 KILOMETERS FROM THE AGRICULTURAL FIELD."

"What are the chances that Hunters will be waiting for us when we get there?"

"UNKNOWN, BUT VERY HIGH. THEY ARE CERTAINLY IN THE AREA AND WILL SEE AND HEAR THE SHIP ON ITS FINAL APPROACH. IF THEY ARE NOT WAITING, THEY WILL CONVERGE QUICKLY."

"Faster than last time?"

"DEFINITELY."

Jeff looked at Ariel again. She hadn't moved. Behind them, Derec seemed to be asleep. Neither of them would run very far.

CHAPTER 13
INTO THE MOUNTAINS

Wolruf had been trotting up and down the blocks, growing more frantic in her search for a moving vehicle of some kind. Inside the buildings, most machinery ran smoothly without even the presence of function robots. Finally she spotted a small wheeled function robot rolling at a good clip along a side street.

She took off at a dead run for it. Oblivious to her, it turned a corner and disappeared from sight. By the time she got there, it had gained more distance on her and was angling across a wide street. None of the slidewalks would take her that way.

She was slowing down, about to give up, when it abruptly changed direction toward a doorway. The door opened automatically, timed so that the function robot did not have to slow down at all. She forced herself to hurry on.

Wolruf was not in particularly good condition. Since joining Derec, she had been starved on several occasions, overfed on others, injured, and—like all of them except Mandelbrot—sometimes overworked and stressed to her limit. She was now basically healthy, but she had not had exercise like this for a long time.

Then she saw the function robot emerge from the doorway and zip across the boulevard again. It mounted a slidewalk this time and actually came back toward her. Panting heavily, she turned and ran for the slidewalk, angling toward a likely intersection point with it as it rolled along the moving slidewalk.

She got a better look at it as she converged on it. It was only about a meter square and two meters high. The wheels, as she had first identified them, proved to be a bed of spheres that gave it the capacity to alter direction without turning its body.

The body of the little robot was smooth and featureless. Wolruf had no chance of catching it if it passed her again, considering how exhausted she was. As she closed with it, she leaped, scrabbled for a hold, and managed to hang on.

The robot immediately slowed down. It did not stop, however, so she clung to its body and rode. At least her body heat had left the stationary surfaces on the ground. Now she had to catch her breath and hope this thing didn't carry her right into the view of a Hunter.

She realized that she had no idea what this was programmed to do. From its size and what she had seen, she guessed it was a courier of some sort, perhaps for small parts and tools. That might account for its slowing down in response to her weight, but not otherwise reacting. Right now, though, it was taking her away from the mountains that she desperately wanted to enter.

Suddenly it moved onto the stationary shoulder, slowed down, and came to a halt. She looked around, puzzled, and saw nothing. Then it started across the street.

She raised up and looked off to her side, which was now the way they were going. A large Hunter robot was striding down another slidewalk toward them. When it had seen her, it had obviously instructed the function robot to move toward it.

Wolruf jumped off the function robot and ran the other way, turning the first corner she reached. A slidewalk here would carry her in the direction she wanted, so she mounted it and went into a trot. At the next corner, she jumped off and turned another corner. The Hunter could move faster than she could, and she was tiring rapidly even after her brief rest riding the courier, or whatever that thing had been.

She had only moments left to think of something.

With no other recourse, she headed straight for the mountains, only a few blocks away. Another slidewalk would help, though of course the Hunter could ride it, too. As the boulevard bordering the foothills came into view, she looked behind her.

The Hunter was in full view and running down the moving slidewalk toward her.

She glanced quickly in both directions as she crossed the

boulevard. The street was empty as far as she could see on both sides. Then she was across it, darting among the trunks of tall trees.

She climbed the slope as fast as she could, ducking under branches and dodging bushes. The forest showed signs of the careful Robot City planning: The types of trees and bushes varied with a certain regularity, as did their sizes. Planting had been done with the long view in mind, both of harvesting and of soil usage.

As she bent low to pass under the arching branches of a large bush shaped something like a simple water fountain, she realized that she just might gain some ground here. Her size was a considerable advantage in the close maze of growth. As far as she had seen, the Hunters were uniformly among the tallest and bulkiest of the humanoid robots.

If only she could gain enough time to rest.

Derec awakened in the berth, at first puzzled by his surroundings. Then he remembered, vaguely, that Jeff and Ariel had somehow reclined his seat into an entirely flat position so that he could rest more comfortably. He lay quietly for a while, staring at the ceiling.

Thankfully, he had not experienced any of those wild dreams in some time. Their weirdness was frightening. Yet he felt worn out, even after sleeping.

Maybe he had been having those nightmares and not remembering them. The chemfets were growing inside him like an organic parasite. Their symptoms also evolved, like those of a disease. Not having those dreams, or at least not remembering them, was yet another sign of how far beyond the early stages his condition had advanced.

He reached over to one of the screens and sent it back up into the ceiling. When he rose up on one shoulder to look around, he saw the silhouettes of Jeff and Ariel in the front of the ship. They were turning around at the sound of the wall screens moving.

"Derec?" Ariel said softly. "How are you feeling?"

He cleared his throat and swung his legs over the side of the bed, hiding the pains in all his muscles.

"Derec?" She repeated, moving to him.

"A little better," said Derec. He started to stand, then decided not to take the risk of falling.

"I had one of my . . . memory fugues again."

"Really? How bad was it?" He looked up at her in surprise. "You haven't had one for some time."

"I don't know how bad it was."

"What?"

"Jeff told me I was just staring at nothing. And I don't remember it at all."

"Maybe you phased back to the time before I had your new memory developing again. Right into that empty period. Anyhow, it's over." He sighed. "As for me, my symptoms have been . . . changing."

She looked at him without speaking.

Derec knew she understood that meant he was getting worse.

"We have to land," said Jeff, joining them. "I can't do anything for either one of you if . . . if something happens again."

"Then you've heard from Mandelbrot?" Derec asked.

"No. We haven't. But our fuel is running low."

"All we're using here is enough for life support," said Ariel.

"And for evasive changes in direction. Landing and takeoff will also use a lot." Derec nodded. "All right. Do you have any plan of action?"

"Yeah, but it's not very good. Basically, we land on one of the big boulevards the ship computer has identified as a site and drive this thing to the edge of the mountains. Then we run for it."

"I'm . . . not going to be running very fast."

Jeff nodded.

"And the central computer can study our final approach and tell the Hunters where we're likely to land."

"The Hunters will be waiting at the landing site," Ariel agreed. "But we can gain some ground on them by taxiing in the ship right to the foothills."

"And then?" Derec said pointedly.

Jeff and Ariel just looked at each other.

"All right," said Derec. "We can't stay up here. We'll have to take our chances."

Wolruf darted under another of those thick, fountain-shaped bushes and paused to rest. She had had two glimpses of her pursuit down the slope; at least two Hunters were now behind her. Though her crooked path had made calculating distance difficult, she did not think they had gained ground on her.

She continued to study the ground around her, as she did when fleeing. Finally, here, she located what she had expected to find all along. The robots were too efficient and well-organized to cultivate a forest without them.

A small metal stud protruded from the ground in front of her. She studied it carefully, poking at it with her stubby, sausage-like fingers. Then she began to look around in the dirt again.

A high-pitched whine caught her attention. It was faint at first, but growing louder quickly, turning into a wail from the sky. Human ears could not have heard it at this distance, but she could, and that meant the robots easily could. She could not see upward clearly from the forest floor, but the sound of the *Minneapolis* in shuttle mode was unmistakable to her sensitive ears.

She waited, quivering with tension. As she listened, the ship obviously came to land safely somewhere in the urban area. Then it grew so faint that she wasn't sure if it had stopped or not. After a moment, it began to grow louder again.

She understood that the humans had decided to risk getting to the crop field however they could. That meant she could help them, if the Hunters did not come upon her too soon. She finally located a small rock in the dirt around her and began striking it against the little metal post with glancing blows.

At first she couldn't hit it at the right angle. Then, even after she had produced a few sparks, she found all of them flying away from the metal. Eventually, however, one of the sparks fell back onto the small metal post itself.

Instantly, one of the highly sensitive Robot City sensors responded to the heat by producing a fine spray of water, no more than a meter high. Greater heat would undoubtedly have triggered a stronger spray; however, this would be good enough for her purposes. The sprinklers would dampen the ground behind her, eliminating the body heat that the Hunters had been tracking.

She looked around, blinking against the spray. Other

sprinklers near her had also been triggered, as far as she could see. As always, these robots had designed their system efficiently.

The *Minneapolis* had come to a halt some distance to her left, according to the sound, at the bottom of the foothills. She wanted to join the humans again, but did not dare. They could lose their pursuit now in the sprinkled area, but the Hunters behind her were too close. She might just lead them right to the others.

She took a deep breath and darted away from the bush, looking for rocks, roots, and other hard surfaces to step on. The Hunters could no longer follow her heat, but they could see footprints. She ran on up the slope, away from the crop field.

As Wolruf had surmised, the *Minneapolis* had landed safely at a site surrounded by Hunter robots and had successfully driven through the crowd down the boulevard straight to the base of the mountains. As soon as it had stopped, the door had opened and the ladder had extended. Jeff and Ariel were helping Derec out the door when he stopped on the top rung of the ladder.

"Hold it," said Derec. "Ship computer!"

"STANDING BY."

"You have a record of all the Hunters who were waiting for us at the landing site just a minute ago?"

"AFFIRMATIVE. ALL ROBOTS PRESENT AT THE SITE WERE RECORDED ON THE VIEWSCREEN TAPES."

"Chase them," said Derec. "As long as you can do so without endangering the ship. Pursue them up and down any boulevards big enough for you."

"CLARIFY."

"Make them think you're going to run them down—in fact, do so if you can. The Third Law requires them to take care of themselves, so keep as many of them distracted and out of the mountains as you can. Got it?" Derec indulged in a grin.

"ACKNOWLEDGED."

"Let's go."

Jeff and Ariel walked on each side of him, holding his arms draped over their shoulders as they hurried awkwardly to the edge of the forested hills. All three of them had to watch the ground right in front of them and each other's feet just to keep from stumbling.

"This is insane," Derec said through his teeth. "We can't even outrun an Auroran striped hastifer. How are we going to get away from the Hunters this way?"

"Better than a crash landing with no fuel for shuttle mode," panted Jeff.

"It's getting worse," said Ariel. "Yuck. I'm getting wet. It must be raining."

Derec jerked his head up and looked at the brush and trees around them. "Really? No, it's not raining. . . . Look— sprinklers!" He grinned. *"Sprinklers!"*

"What—" Ariel paused to edge around the trunk of a tree, as she was still tangled in Derec's arm. "What are you so happy about?"

"The Hunters have been using heat sensors to track us. We have a chance now."

"Mud," said Jeff. He turned his head to one side and ducked under a branch. "That's our next problem. We have to watch our footsteps or they'll just follow those."

Derec pulled his arm free from Ariel. "And I've got some adrenaline flowing again. I'm loosening up. Come on—as long as I'm really worked up, I can move." He pulled away from Jeff, too, trying to hide the extreme pains he still felt.

Jeff studied his face. "Whatever you say. But if you really need help, say so, all right?"

"Yeah, yeah. Come on."

Jeff led the way up the slope. The forest grew thicker very quickly and then remained almost uniformly the same, probably the result of precise robot planting. Derec followed him, straining not to show how much difficulty he was having. Still, Jeff tended to gain on him, while Ariel was always moving up right behind him.

As Derec struggled on, one fact kept returning to his thoughts. Dr. Avery had done this to him—and Derec had never done anything to him. His anger served to fire him, to keep him moving, to force him onward. Dr. Avery would not escape.

Jeff stepped onto a ridge of white rock and stopped, breathing hard. Derec came up and joined him, but collapsed into a sitting position. Ariel stood next to him.

"That agricultural park, or whatever you want to call it, is that way," said Jeff, nodding at an angle over the mountains. "According to the viewscreen, there are passes on each side of us."

Derec looked up at him, but was too out of breath to speak. He just nodded.

"It looks like these rocks extend across this foothill for some distance," Jeff went on. "They'll take us toward either pass. I think we should stay on this ridge for as long as we can to avoid leaving footprints."

"Maybe the ship really slowed down a few Hunters," Ariel said when she had the breath.

"We can hope so," said Jeff. "But we'd better get going."

Derec struggled to get up. "Okay," he said huskily.

They started again, more slowly this time.

CHAPTER 14
THE AGRICULTURAL PARK

Twilight had fallen on the mountain pass by the time Derec plodded after Jeff and Ariel to its far side. They waited for him to catch up and he leaned an arm across Ariel's shoulders when he arrived. Together, the three of them looked out over the green valley below.

The valley was divided into many different fields, all of them tended by function robots. The hoes were easily identified, even at this great distance. There were others moving about, some clipping and spraying. The lower slopes leading into the valley were terraced and cultivated, also.

"This has to be the place," said Derec. "Robots just don't need this stuff."

"I agree," said Jeff. "This is Avery's grocery store. Or at least, his produce market. If he has livestock, they must be somewhere else."

"They would require different care and processing." Derec nodded. "And these robots are too efficient to put this here and Avery a thousand kilometers away. I'm betting he's in the neighborhood, someplace."

"And we made it," said Ariel. "This far, anyway."

"We couldn't help leaving a few footprints here and there," said Jeff. "And those Hunter robots may have sensors I can't even imagine. They don't have to stop for the night, either."

"They'll spot all kinds of details we left behind," said Derec.

"Broken branches and things like that. As much as I hate to say this . . . we'd better move on."

"Some of them probably went to the other pass," Ariel pointed out. "There won't be as many behind us."

"That pass leads to this valley, too," said Jeff. "We might just meet them coming the other way."

Ariel shook her head. "You're so optimistic. Come on."

They started down the slope and soon entered the cultivated rows of some plant that none of them could identify. It grew in a straight stalk with stiff, narrow leaves angling sharply upward, roughly three meters high. The stalks were planted close together, forcing them to walk in single file between the rows.

Jeff looked back over his shoulder nervously. "We're leaving a track even I could follow. Look down."

Derec looked. The soil was freshly turned and damp. Their footprints were clear and deep. "These robots must hoe and water constantly."

"It hasn't gotten any darker," said Ariel. She looked up at the sky. "It should have by now."

"Lights must have come on," Derec said. "I can't tell from where, though. The function robots here may need some to work at night. Or else this is growth light of some kind for the crops."

Jeff was pushing experimentally between two stalks in one of the rows. "Come on. We can squeeze between these. We have to break up our trail a little."

The others followed him through. The next row was identical to the previous one as far as Derec could see. They walked down it for a while, then found another spot where they could push through into the next row down into the valley.

"Up there," said Derec, pointing. "We have to catch it. Come on!"

Some distance ahead, a function robot was moving away from them at a moderate speed. The body of this robot was roughly a cube two meters on a side. It seemed to advance on a bed of vertical spikes that chewed into the ground as it walked forward, thereby hoeing the soil it covered. At intervals, it stopped and sent tentacles out to each side that stabbed into the earth in the rows of crops and pulled out small plants into its own body.

Jeff ran for it. As Ariel tried to help Derec along, he glanced at the rows of crops as they passed. Apparently that stabbing motion cut the roots of unwanted plants that had grown up between the desired crops. The weeds were drawn into the function robot, ground up, and deposited through the bottom to be left behind as instant compost. He could see the tiny bits here and there in the soil now that he was looking.

"I got it but I don't see any way to stop it," Jeff called. He was now sitting on the body of the hoer, facing backward.

"Stupid thing," said Ariel. "I wish it had a positronic brain so we could order it around."

"No," said Derec, struggling after her. "It could also report to the Hunters, in that case."

The hoer would not wait for them, but every time it stopped to weed they gained on it a little. At last they were able to climb on board with Jeff, where they sat awkwardly on its crowded top.

"Now we just need some luck," said Jeff. "If this thing stays out of the sight of the Hunters until it takes a few turns here and there, they won't be able to track us easily after all. All the rows have the same appearance after these things go through them."

"I can use the rest," said Derec. "But we have to figure out where Avery is while we can. I didn't see any buildings in this valley when we came in."

"I didn't either," said Jeff, shaking his head.

"Then what else do you remember?" Ariel asked. "From your father? Anything."

"I thought about it while we were climbing up the mountain," said Jeff. "But I didn't have breath to talk. You remember how I told you that Avery wanted to know about cultures that could endure?"

Ariel nodded. Derec was alert but too tired to respond.

"My father told him that two groups exist even now, in space, that are descended in a straight line from ancient Earth. Both of them have continued to evolve in Spacer communities, but their longevity really got Avery's attention."

"What were they?" Ariel asked.

"One is the Spacer minority culture descended from China

through a couple of migrations on Earth. The other is the Spacer Jewish communities."

"What did he want to know about them?" Ariel made a face. "I don't see how this is going to help us find him here."

Jeff shrugged. "I do recall that he didn't care about their details. My father tried to tell him that both these cultures had continued to evolve in space. He even said that in many ways they were totally unrecognizable from their ancestral Earth cultures. But all Avery wanted to know was how they had survived as specific entities."

That was consistent, Derec thought to himself. The guy only cared about his own project and what he could do to improve it.

"He was looking for clues for Robot City," Ariel said. "To make it endure across the centuries. That's what he was researching with Professor Leong. He needed to program cultural values into the city. But we haven't really seen very much of that."

Derec forced himself to speak. "I'm sure that he reprogrammed the city while we were on Earth. I think after the incidents surrounding the performance of *Hamlet,* the robot creativity scared him. He couldn't have his robots committing crimes against each other."

"The arts aren't the only part of culture," said Jeff.

"What do you mean?" Ariel asked.

Derec shifted slightly so that he could hear Jeff better. The hoer moved right along, still hoeing and weeding. The sky above them now looked dark, but a soft glow of light from somewhere illuminated the rows of crops.

"My father gave Avery two reasons for the cultural survival of those groups while they were on Earth. One is that the original cultures had very strong family units that passed values on. The other is that, outside of their native countries, both groups on Earth experienced limited assimilation as minorities and often faced prejudice from the majority culture."

"But only on Earth?" Ariel said.

"That's right. Modern Spacer families aren't personally close the way families used to be, I guess. And now the ethnicities are from one planet to another, or Spacer versus Earth."

"My mother didn't like Solarians," said Ariel. "They program their robots funny or something." She smiled. "She told me a joke once that went—"

"How could Avery have used that information?" Derec asked firmly, stopping her with a hand on her arm.

"Come to think of it," said Ariel, "how can these minorities still exist if the original reasons for their endurance no longer do? That doesn't make sense."

"I'm not sure," said Jeff. "But on Aurora, I still look different. That always kept me distinct. And, you know, my father took more interest in me than my friends' fathers. That's why he dragged me out to meet Avery, remember?"

"I think I see," said Ariel. "Maybe some of these tendencies still exist to a degree."

"At least in comparison to the majority cultures on the planet." Jeff nodded.

They all clutched for a hold on the hoer as it reached a perpendicular row and made a right-angle turn without slowing down. It made another right turn at the next row and started down the direction it had just come on the previous one. They could see a long way ahead of them.

So could the Hunters, if they looked down the right row.

Derec was uncomfortable with this talk of families and fathers and sons. He hadn't had any family to speak of since he had awakened with amnesia.

"We still have to find Avery in this valley or this mountain range or somewhere," said Derec with annoyance. "What are we going to do about that?"

"Just one more thing," said Jeff. "My father told Avery that two major events changed both these cultures in ancient times. One was moving from the so-called Old World of Earth to the United States."

"What difference would that make?" Ariel asked. "They were still on Earth."

"He said that while prejudice didn't vanish there, these two cultures were part of a nation of immigrants and their descendants for the first time. They were a fundamental part of these societies even while maintaining their identities."

"What was the other event?" She asked.

"Going into space. The same situation occurred again with the settling of Spacer worlds. Being an Auroran, say, is now more important than one's Earth ancestors. As demonstrated by your mother's attitude toward Solarians."

Ariel nodded thoughtfully.

"So what does all this get us?" Derec demanded. "Robots never did have this kind of identity, anyhow. What does this have to do with Robot City? And finding Dr. Avery?"

"Now, look!" Jeff whirled on him. "You're the one who started asking me what I remember. I'm just telling you. If you don't want to hear it, don't ask me."

Ariel grabbed both their arms. *"Robots,"* she whispered.

Far in the distance ahead of them, the silhouettes of humanoid robots were moving from right to left, down the valley slope, across their open row.

Wolruf gathered her legs under her and leaped from a small rock to a fallen branch large enough to hold her. She landed on it on all fours and hung on till she got her balance. This forest had very few fallen branches, or loose matter of any kind.

The robots obviously cleared the forest floor frequently. She had seen a few function robots in the distance but had kept clear of them. She didn't want the Hunters sending any more orders to function robots that would help them capture her.

Still, she had managed to minimize the footprints she left behind. A fairly small area had been sprinkled by the sensor she had triggered and she had left it before the sprinklers quit operating. She wondered how long they had continued to run.

She hoped they had remained on for some time. If they had sprayed long enough, then the water eventually would not only have eliminated the body heat of her footprints on the ground, but also would have washed away the visual traces.

That and the difficulty the big Hunters would have in moving through the crowded forest might account for their falling behind. When they had lost her trail, they probably would have had to resort to a pattern search to pick it up again, and that would cost them time.

She stayed on the branch to catch her breath. Her memory of the terrain on the ship viewscreen was clear enough, but she wasn't sure exactly where she was. Nor was she sure of what to do.

So far, she had been angling up the slope and away from the

pass that the humans had been near, certain that they were heading there. Anything she could do to draw Hunters away from them would be a contribution. She also remembered that another pass led into the valley somewhere in this direction.

She was torn between two impulses, with no way to know which would better serve the cause of Derec's getting to Avery before Avery's robots got to him. If she got to the pass and joined the humans, they could work together as a team again and perhaps accomplish more. However, that would mean leading the Hunters following her right back toward them again.

This was not getting her anywhere.

She could not afford to rest anywhere too long, even now. After balancing along the fallen branch as far as she could, she jumped off to a patch of ground that looked firm. From there, she stepped on the top of an exposed tree root, grabbed a low-hanging branch, and swung over to a small rock.

Then she paused to look back, wondering if this was worth the effort. If the Hunters came up quickly, their heat sensors would tell them where she had been. Now, however, she was hoping that they were too far behind to use those sensors effectively. If the traces of her body heat subsided before they arrived, minimizing her visual track could be critical.

She continued to move along this way. It was a gamble, but probably worth it. If she could actually lose the Hunters, then she could look for the humans in the valley without endangering them further. In order to know, however, she would have to double back at some point and actually watch the Hunters in action.

That might be too risky. Still undecided, she fled on up the slope, still moving roughly in the direction of the pass. Once she got there, she could make her final decision on whether to enter it or not.

Since the hoer was moving down the row toward the humanoid robots, its passengers had no choice but to get off and go the other way. Derec was surprised that the robots had not looked down the row already and spotted them, but apparently they had not. As before, he followed Jeff and preceded Ariel, all three of them now crawling along the damp earth so that the body of the hoer would block them from view.

Before long, they reached the perpendicular row they had seen a short time before. It ran parallel with the one the humanoid robots were taking in single file to go farther down into the valley. Derec stopped there, breathing hard, unable to go on.

"Derec?" Ariel crawled up beside him. "Jeff, wait."

Jeff looked back over his shoulder and then came back. He watched Derec for a minute and shook his head. "I don't know what to do. We can't just stop."

Derec coughed and shook his head in frustration. He wanted to speak and didn't have the breath for it yet. Quickly, he pointed in a stabbing motion in the direction of the humanoids.

Ariel turned to look. "They aren't coming yet. At least, I don't see anybody."

"No," Derec wheezed. "That's not what I mean." He paused again, still breathing hard. His head was spinning dizzily.

"We could try supporting you between us again," said Jeff. "But we can only do that by standing up and walking."

"Wait, wait." Derec inhaled deeply and looked up at both of

111

them. "Those aren't Hunters. I'm sure of it."

"Really?" Ariel scooted closer to him. "Derec, are you sure? You're not exactly in the best condition."

"Hunters wouldn't just pass by like that without even looking down the row. They can't be Hunters."

"Makes sense to me," said Jeff slowly. "So who are they, then? And what are they doing in this valley?"

"I was thinking about that, too," said Derec. "I think they're migrating. They're following that mysterious migration programming we told you we heard about."

"So the only danger from them," said Jeff, "is that if they notice us, the Hunters can ask them where we were. Otherwise they won't bother us?"

"That's right," said Derec. "But we can also find out where they're going—where their assembly point is. And what this whole operation is for."

"Now?" Ariel said, making a face. "Derec, we don't have much time left to find Avery. We can't just go wandering off—"

"No! Don't you understand? This migration thing is Avery's doing. If we can figure it out, maybe we'll find him. He's behind it all, and it's obviously very important to him."

"That sounds awfully risky," said Jeff.

"Look at me! Risky? I don't have much time left!" Derec spoke forcefully, but was too weak to speak loudly now. "I think we've talked long enough. What are we going to *do?*"

"That row is full of robot footsteps, too," said Ariel. "Ours would be camouflaged some."

"It is something to go on," Jeff said slowly.

"I wish Mandelbrot was here," said Ariel. "And poor Wolruf, running around in Robot City with him. I wonder where they are. I hope they're all right."

"We can't worry about them," said Derec. "We can't help them directly now, anyway. If we get to Avery, we can make him ease up on them, too. We have to concentrate on Avery."

"That's right," said Jeff. "The truth is, they can probably take care of themselves better then we can, especially Mandelbrot. And Derec seems to be the one Dr. Avery is after."

"I've been putting some ideas together," said Derec. "While we were crawling in the mud back there, just now."

"All right," said Jeff, "let's hear 'em. If they aren't going to come after us, we have a few minutes."

"Unless the Hunters get here too," added Ariel.

"Listen," said Derec. "Avery learned from Professor Leong that the two most important forces behind cultural longevity are passing on values and maintaining a distinct identity. Right?"

"Sure," said Jeff.

"So passing values down is not a problem with robots; they're just programmed. They can process information much faster and keep more of it accessible than humans."

"No argument there," said Jeff.

Ariel nodded. "And all along, we've seen that these Avery robots are different from any other sort. They behave in a different way. Their programming must have been special from the beginning."

"Exactly," said Derec. "Both of those facts fit perfectly. And the isolation of Robot City prevents it from being altered by cultures from the outside."

Jeff nodded. "Its location is still a secret."

"So Avery really took those two lessons to heart and used them to form Robot City," said Ariel.

"One big question remains," said Derec. "What values did he program into them?"

"Efficiency," said Jeff.

"Harmony," said Ariel. "Both of those. A kind of idealism. Remember when they gave us their provisional Laws of Humanics, for ideal human behavior? Robot City was supposed to be a kind of utopia. We already knew that."

"But now we know what kind—on what basis." Derec nodded with excitement. He now felt a surge of energy again that animated him once more.

"I'm starting to get the idea," said Jeff. "What do you want to do about it?"

"Challenge the system," said Derec. "Force it to malfunction, or at least make it look like it is."

"To make Avery show himself," Ariel said. "All right. I get it. But . . . how?"

"We have to present the system—that is, the central computer—with irrational events," said Derec. "Look—the Supervisors originally needed us to solve a crime against a human when we first arrived. The system here has that weak point."

"And we never did figure out who the victim was, either," said Ariel. She shivered. "He looked just like you. That still gives me the creeps, even now."

Derec said nothing. When he had first entered Avery's office he had come across some mysterious information about the dead man that he had never shared with Ariel. This was no time to launch into that topic.

Jeff looked at her in surprise. They had never told him that part of their story.

"Well, for the moment, forget it," said Derec sharply. "One crisis at a time. The reason we arranged the *Hamlet* performance was also to accomplish something that the robots weren't ready to handle."

"I see what you're getting at," said Jeff. "That's a weak point in the system. A utopia isn't supposed to have crimes and these Avery robots can't really handle them."

"Exactly," said Derec. "I think we have to commit a few crimes against humanoid robots. We aren't bound by the Laws of Robotics and Mandelbrot isn't around to interfere if a situation arose that involved the Laws."

Jeff grinned wryly. "Okay . . . let's become criminals. What'll we do first, boss?"

Derec grinned himself, despite his discomfort. "We have to incapacitate a robot."

"Murder one?" Ariel shook her head. "I don't see how. Those heads of theirs are as hard as a ship's hull. We could bonk them on the head and not even get their attention."

All three of them giggled nervously. The tension was broken a little by the hope of taking aggressive action.

"We can't unfasten their bodies, either," said Jeff, still grinning. "No tools. Otherwise, we could just sneak up behind them, power up the tools, and leave a little junkpile behind."

"We could go into business later with used parts," said Ariel. "Discounted Avery robot parts, cheap."

"All right, all right." Derec shook his head. "We don't actually need any physical violence. The first thing we have to do is get over to that other row, so we can look for one robot walking alone. Let's crawl back over there."

It was a very long crawl. Derec had to stop several times on the way to rest. Each time, he worried that the Hunters were going to catch up to them before they could accomplish anything.

Finally they reached the last few tall, leafy stalks before the break in the rows. The three of them huddled at the corner of the row, where Derec could lean forward and look up the slope. Jeff and Ariel sat on his other side, both of them looking around anxiously for Hunters coming from other directions.

"Nothing yet," said Derec. "That gives me time to explain what I have in mind."

"I hope more are coming this way," said Ariel. "What if the bunch going to that assembly point is all there?"

"Good point," said Derec. "Maybe we should follow them. Just keep a look-out behind us—"

"No good," said Jeff. "These rows are absolutely straight. If the Hunters come along, they can look straight down the slope and spot us instantly even from the very opening of the pass."

"We'd better stay here." Ariel settled into a comfortable position. "Derec, tell us what you're planning while we have a chance to talk it over."

"You mentioned their Laws of Humanics." Derec nodded at Ariel.

"I don't remember the exact wording, but their provisional First Law of Humanics was to the effect that humans wouldn't injure another human or let one come to harm through inaction."

"They just rewrote the First Law of Robotics." Jeff shrugged.

"The Second Law of Humanics might help us," said Derec. "It says that humans must only give reasonable orders to a robot and not require anything that would distress it. Their Third Law of Humanics is the best one for us, though. It says that we must not harm a robot or let one come to harm through inaction, unless such harm is needed to help a human or allow a vital order to be carried out."

"How do you want to use them?" Ariel asked.

"We need to violate the Third Law of Humanics and maybe the Second to prove that this isn't a utopia even for robots." Derec looked at them both. "You follow me?"

"So far," said Jeff.

"How do we do that?" Ariel asked.

"Basically, we have to convince our victim that my physical condition is his fault."

"All right." Jeff nodded. "In other words, force it into shutting itself down because it thinks it has violated the First Law. That makes sense to me. We have a better chance of that than of wrestling it to the ground."

"How?" Ariel demanded. "They aren't exactly stupid. They'll know if they've harmed you or not."

"We'll have to play-act a scene," said Derec. "I haven't really figured out the details. Maybe if it thinks it caused you two to attack me, or something like that."

"I hear footsteps," said Jeff.

Derec got down low and carefully looked around the nearest plant, up the slope. A lone humanoid robot was coming down the row. Derec gathered his feet under him and waited.

"What are we supposed to do?" Ariel whispered.

"We'll all have to improvise," he whispered back, gesturing with his hand. "Quiet."

Just as the robot reached him, Derec threw himself forward to clutch at the robot's legs.

"Stop!" Derec called hoarsely, looking up at the robot's face. He didn't have to fake his pain any, but he gave vent to it in his facial expression. "You hurt me."

The robot stopped, looking down at him. "If I did so, it was inadvertant. I apologize." The robot reached down to take Derec under its arms and lift him.

At the contact, Derec let out a scream and went limp. He slid out of the robot's grasp to lie on the ground face up.

"You've killed him!" Ariel screamed, jumping up. "You murderer, you've killed him!"

Derec struggled not to smile at her vehemence. He lay with his eyes open, so he could follow what was happening.

"Looks that way," said Jeff. "Maybe you ought to shut down, pal. You can't go around violating the First Law like that."

The robot was visibly quivering. "I did not harm him. Our contact was minimal and of very low impact. This is a misunderstanding. I will help him find care."

"No! Don't you touch him!" Ariel shouted, waving her arms wildly. "You'll do it again."

"Humans cannot die more than once," said the robot. "Besides, he is not dead."

"He's in very bad shape," said Jeff. "It's your fault. Do you understand that?"

Derec started grimacing and writhing in pain, with relatively little play-acting required.

"I . . . could . . . not have harmed him," the robot insisted. "My contact . . . with him . . . would not damage him."

The robot's hesitation revealed his doubt. Derec was encouraged. They just had to keep at it.

"And no reporting to the central computer," Jeff said suddenly. "I almost forgot. You haven't done that, have you?"

"No . . . I was . . . distracted."

"Well, don't. That's an order. Second Law. Got it?" Jeff demanded, pointing a finger at him.

"Yes. . . ."

"Don't you think you ought to shut down?" Ariel said forcefully, her hands on her hips. "After doing this to him?"

"I am . . . not . . . convinced."

"If you won't shut down," said Jeff, "then we'll have beat him up ourselves. And that will definitely be your fault."

"That . . . is illogical."

"Are you going to shut down or not?" Ariel demanded.

"No . . . I will not. . . ."

"Wait a minute," Derec wheezed, trying to sound as injured as he could. "Do you admit that you are in doubt about this?"

"Yes."

"Then you should at least agree to come with us where we can discuss it further."

"That's right," said Jeff. "You can't argue that, can you?"

"Good idea," said Ariel, looking up the slope. "We, uh, don't want to be interrupted."

"Carry me," Derec said to the robot. "Who are you, anyway? And what do you do?"

"I . . . am Pei," said the robot, with somewhat less hesitation. "My task is Architectural Designer." He bent down and gently picked up Derec. "Where . . . shall we go?"

"We want to be out of sight of this row," said Jeff. "But not too far. Uh, let's cross that row and go to the other side."

"Very well," said Pei. "However, we cannot go out of sight of this row unless we go some distance. I see a slight dip in the row ahead that may suffice if we all sit on the ground."

"Perfect," said Ariel. "C'mon, let's hurry."

With Pei carrying Derec, the group moved quickly for the first time since they had left the *Minneapolis*. As they walked, Derec relaxed a little and closed his eyes. It was a relief to rest again, even for a few moments before they stopped.

Pei set him down with extreme care. Then the others sat down around him on the damp, soft soil.

"Explain . . . my transgression . . . of the First Law," said Pei. He began quivering a little more again.

Derec, lying with eyes closed, felt guilty about distressing the robot this way. He reminded himself, however, that the same robot was under Avery programming. He would turn them all in if the central computer or the Hunters knew he was with them and instructed him to do so.

Besides, he could be repaired or reprogrammed later with no lasting damage. *I can't,* Derec thought. He opened his eyes.

"You harmed me," Derec asserted as firmly as he could. "Shut yourself down."

"At least for a while, you know, until you can be checked," said Ariel. "That's standard procedure, isn't it?"

Her phrasing sounded lame to Derec. He realized that she felt guilty about this, too.

"I . . . must be . . . convinced," said Pei.

CHAPTER 16

TO CHALLENGE UTOPIA

Derec suddenly acted on another impulse. With effort, he rolled onto his side and got his aching legs under him. Then he launched himself at Jeff without warning, reaching for Jeff's throat as if he wanted to strangle him.

Just as he got his hands around Jeff's neck, Pei gently grasped his wrists. Even at the slight pressure, Derec screamed and fell back, drawing his arms away with his hands limp. Then he collapsed to the ground with his eyes closed.

"You did it again!" Jeff cried, not too loudly.

"You've really hurt him this time," said Ariel.

"This is an acceptable move," said Pei. "I have prevented greater harm to this human by making a less harmful move to the one attacking him. No violation of the First Law has been made." His confidence was returning.

Derec opened his eyes, not otherwise moving.

"Uh. . . ." Jeff looked helplessly at Ariel.

"You overdid it," said Ariel excitedly. "Look at him. That's not called for!"

"That's right," Jeff declared. "Stopping him with reasonable force is all right, but this is something else!"

Pei looked down at Derec. "I . . . could not . . . have hurt him. I . . . was . . . gentle."

"Not gentle enough," Ariel wailed. "That's twice you've hurt him. You just don't understand how fragile humans are."

"That's right," said Jeff eagerly. "That's the problem. If

119

you've never had contact with humans before, that explains it. Suppose you shut down till your judgement is fixed up. Or something." He shrugged lamely at Ariel.

"It's your judgement," Ariel agreed, "that must be faulty at the core, so to speak. You can't risk harming a human because of that, can you?"

"Perhaps . . . you have . . . a point." Pei's voice grew faint and he froze in place.

"Pei, are you awake?" Ariel asked cautiously.

"Pei, if you can hear me, I order you to say so," said Jeff.

When Derec didn't hear anything, he forced himself up on one elbow. "Hey, it finally worked."

"I guess it did," said Ariel.

"Then it should work again," said Jeff. "And now that we know what it takes, we can refine our scenario."

"Let's get back over to that row they're taking," said Derec. "Can you help me up?"

Yet again, Jeff and Ariel helped him to his feet and supported his arms over their shoulders. The trio shuffled back to the one row that these humanoid robots were using for their trip down into the valley. There Derec once more sank to the ground.

Jeff and Ariel this time paced nervously between the high stalks on each side of the furrow.

"Maybe we ought to move on," said Ariel. "Isn't one mugged robot enough? I mean, one murdered human and one murdered robot caused major crises in Robot City before."

"That's a good point," said Jeff. "Maybe we could drag him over here where the next migrating robot will be sure to find him. But we could move on, keep ahead of the Hunters."

"I can't help you drag him," said Derec. "And he's pretty big. I doubt the two of you could get him all the way over here."

Jeff ran a hand through his straight black hair and sighed. "You're right. It's been a rough day already, and we may have a lot more running ahead."

"One more robot," said Derec. "That's all we need."

"What are you talking about?" Ariel demanded. "If we just stand here and wait for the Hunters, all this has been for nothing anyway. We have to get out of here."

"Just one more robot. Instead of mugging it, we'll just make sure it sees Pei, back there. Then we'll move on."

"Well . . . all right," said Ariel. "We'll wait a little while. But if nothing comes before long, we're leaving anyway. Agreed?"

"Fair enough," said Derec. "But remember, it has to be one robot walking alone. I'm pretty sure that trying to fool more than one would be tougher because the others will observe and may spot the fraud. Let's not chance that."

More robots did walk down the row before much time had passed, and all of them seemed to be migrating alone in the sense that they were not part of a crew or a team. However, they often came down the row in sight of one or more robots behind them, and Derec did not dare attempt their charade under those circumstances.

"Remember," said Derec, "not that much time has really passed for the Hunters to get here. It just seems longer to us than it has been because we're scared."

"Here comes another one," said Ariel, peeking around the leafy stalk on the corner of the row. "It looks good. I don't see anyone behind him yet."

Jeff moved next to her to look. "Hey, Derec. I think this is it. We've got another one."

"Finally. All right. Just before he gets here, I'll throw myself on the ground and you jump on me." He smiled wryly. "Not too hard, okay? I'm half dead already."

"Derec, don't talk that way—" Ariel began.

"Hey—wait a minute," said Jeff. "I know that robot. It's . . . what did I name him? Oh, yeah. Hey, Can Head!" Jeff stepped out in front of the robot.

The robot stopped suddenly, looking at him in some surprise. "Are you addressing me?"

"Identify yourself," said Jeff.

"I am Energy Pack Maintenance Foreman 3928," said the robot. "I am following migration programming. Please allow me to pass."

"That sounds right. I'm sure it's you." Jeff nodded, studying the robot's eyeslit and general shape.

"Jeff, what are you doing?" Derec asked.

"I knew this character," said Jeff. "I even gave him a second name. He was very cooperative."

"They've all been reprogrammed," Ariel said urgently. "We're sure of it, remember? He won't retain anything from when you were here before. Let's get on with it."

"C'mon, pal, remember?" Jeff grinned. "You will also answer to Can Head, won't you?"

"Yes. I also answer to Can Head."

Ariel laughed in surprise, stifling it with a hand over her mouth.

"There!" Jeff grinned at her and Derec.

Derec shrugged at Ariel.

"I'm the human who was in a robot body before," said Jeff to Can Head. "I gave you that name and now I have further instructions. First, don't contact the central computer with any of this. Got it?" He winked down at Derec. "I used to say that on my last trip here, too."

"Understood," said Can Head.

"Do you remember me?" Jeff asked.

"No."

"You don't?" Jeff started. "Then why do you still answer to Can Head?"

"I've got it," said Derec. "All the robots of Robot City were reprogrammed through the central core, but their identities and designations were not changed. That would be counterproductive for Avery because the central computer still has to be able to contact and recognize all the different robots."

"I guess," said Jeff. "I'm disappointed. I thought I had an old friend, here."

"That's nothing," said Derec. "You should have seen the greeting we got from Euler, an old friend of ours. He's the one who sent the Hunters after us."

"Anyhow, he's being cooperative," said Jeff. "Maybe we don't need our scenario." He turned to Can Head. "We must show you something. However, before we do, we request your help—no, we *require* your help under the First Law."

"How may I help?" Can Head asked.

"This human is Derec and he is extremely ill. We—"

"He looks it," said Can Head.

"A comedian," Derec muttered.

"We need you to carry him for us for a while," said Jeff.

"Why?"

"We . . . are being followed by those who would do further harm," said Ariel, speaking slowly to get the right phrases.

"Exactly," said Derec.

"Who are they?" Can Head asked.

"We can't say," said Jeff. "But it doesn't matter, does it? Harm is harm under the First Law."

"I am under high-priority programming to migrate," said Can Head. "To violate it, I must understand the urgency of the potential harm."

"Hold it," said Derec. "Let's combine the two. Look—you see where the ground dips over there?"

"Yes."

"An inactive humanoid robot is lying there. After you take us to safety, we want you to report it to the central computer, but not before. You understand?"

"So far," said Can Head.

"Before you do that, carry me and lead them on an evasive pattern toward your assembly point. That will combine your programming with our needs under the First Law. Can you do that?"

"My programming requires that I migrate directly," said Can Head. He turned to look at the dip in the ground. "A humanoid robot has malfunctioned here?"

"Sort of," said Derec. "It's more like he was mugged."

"Mugged? In the sense of criminal violence?"

"That's what I mean, yeah."

Can Head turned his eyeslit directly down at Derec. "Is this development directly related to the danger you are in?"

"Uh—yes! It is directly related," said Derec. "But we don't need to discuss how. Will you help us or not?"

"I believe this is sufficient reason to take you on an evasive pattern toward my assembly point." Can Head leaned down and picked up Derec with surprising gentleness, even for a robot. "Follow me," he said to Jeff and Ariel.

Derec let out a sigh of relief. As long as they were moving ahead of the Hunters, they had a chance, and an evasive pattern taken by a robot might at least be the equal of the Hunters' ability to solve it. It would be better than their own, at any rate.

He would instruct Can Head to drop them off before he reached his assembly point and to keep his contact with them secret. At that time, he thought sleepily, he could cajole an explanation of the migration programming out of him. Right now, he was just so tired. . . .

He was comforted by the strong, rhythmic stride of Can Head and by the sound of the footsteps of Jeff and Ariel right behind them. News of the mugging of their victim was certain to reach Dr. Avery. What Derec needed now was Mandelbrot. Mandelbrot could contact the central computer and, unlike Can Head and the other Avery robots, he could be trusted to help without these convoluted discussions of the Laws.

Mandelbrot . . . and Wolruf. He drifted off to sleep wondering what had happened to them.

Mandelbrot was standing motionless in a repair facility. The trip here had been a long one, covering a surprisingly long distance. He had been deposited here just a moment before by the helpful robot.

He had successfully evaded the Hunters behind him by dual moves. The first was having that other robot carry him to eliminate his heat trail, and the second was being identified as a malfunctioning robot. Apparently the Hunters, with no reason to believe he was in need of repair, were acting under the assumption that he was still in full flight. He would have to move on before they thought of checking here.

Mandelbrot also had to get out before the repair robots required his identification, and that would be any time now.

At first he had been surprised by being set down and left to wait. The efficiency of the Avery robots had led him to expect immediate handling. As he observed the workings in the repair facility, however, he concluded that Robot City was, as usual, functioning under its own distinctive style of efficiency.

The repair facility was processing a large number of damaged or malfunctioning robots. Mandelbrot guessed from the conversations he overheard through his comlink that migration programming had largely been completed. Apparently only skeleton staffs remained anywhere in Robot City now.

For that reason, most repair facilities had also been shut down. The robots being repaired here were either already assigned to those skeleton staffs or they were being reprogrammed. Those that entered with migration orders had them purged and were placed in a pool to act as reserves for the skeleton staffs instead.

So Robot City intended to function without the migrating robots for an extended period. Further, any robot that did not reach its assembly point within a short time would be reassigned. Mandelbrot concluded that he could not afford to wait here longer at all, or he would risk being reprogrammed and so lost to the humans as a source of help.

Mandelbrot was standing by four other robots. Two were sitting because of mechanical failures that impaired standing or walking. The other two were standing, the extent of their malfunctions not visible. All of them had managed to reach the repair facility alert and functioning just short of one hundred percent.

Mandelbrot observed the entire room for a moment. A couple of humanoid robots assigned to the facility supervised a large number of function robots doing the actual repair work. One function robot was rolling down the row of waiting robots that Mandelbrot was in, observing serial numbers or something with an eye on a long, flexible tentacle.

Mandelbrot turned and walked quickly out of the building. Outside, he mounted a slidewalk and began to run on it toward the mountains, now invisible in the distance. He knew their direction but had to follow his memory of the ship viewscreen for the best route.

"Stop," called a robot on his comlink. "You are malfunctioning and therefore endanger yourself by risking greater malfunctions. This is a Third Law violation that requires you to shut down—"

Mandelbrot broke his reception. Since he was in fine condition, none of that applied. He had known they would see him take off, and he was gambling that they would not place as high a priority on catching him as the Hunters had. At worst, they would assign a Hunter to catch him as a malfunctioned rogue instead of as an intruder involved with Derec.

Ahead, he saw a tunnel stop. Without looking back, he leaped off the slidewalk and ran down the moving ramp to the loading dock. Then he was inside a platform booth and had programmed it to go as close to the mountains as it could take him.

The trip would take some time. He opened his comlink again to reconnoiter.

Two general alerts were coming from the central computer with high priority codes.

One was that Hunters were now seeking a malfunctioning robot who had apparently violated the Third Law by running away from a repair facility. Because the force of the Laws was involved, all humanoid robots were ordered to watch for him. His physical description was given. Since he had escaped from the repair facility before any scanning was done, they had no more to go on than that, but he was distinctive from the Avery robots even by sight.

The second alert was that a mysteriously shut-down humanoid robot had been found in the agricultural park. Nothing was known about the cause. The Supervisors entered an urgent order that any robots with information about this development report it immediately.

Total malfunctions of this kind were extremely rare in Robot City. Mandelbrot was sure that this one called up memories in the minds of the Supervisors, and probably in Avery himself, of the robot murder that Derec had solved here.

Mandelbrot, of course, was not bound by the instruction. He was sure that his human friends were somehow responsible and he was also certain that the Hunters would guess this, as well. Nevertheless, none of them had proof.

Mandelbrot also figured that the Hunters would guess that the rogue robot was the same one they were hunting. It made no difference, since he had to avoid them either way. He now felt the First Law impetus pushing him on, since the Hunters were likely to be closer to the humans than he was.

The platform booth continued to shoot down the tunnel toward the mountains. It was the fastest transportation he had, and it seemed painfully slow.

Derec heard Ariel calling his name. It came out of darkness, out of fog, out of chilly air . . . until he finally opened his eyes and found himself looking up at her with some thick, tall grass waving behind her in the dim glow suffusing the entire valley. He said nothing at first, trying to remember where they were. The surroundings were totally unfamiliar to him.

"Derec, *please* wake up. We have to move again." Her voice was pleading.

"Come on. I'll help you." Jeff got an arm under Derec and pulled him into a sitting position.

"Where are we?" Derec asked, looking around. His voice was dry and hoarse. "What's happened?"

"You fell asleep while Can Head was carrying you," said Ariel. "He's gone now."

"You've been asleep for some time," said Jeff. "It must be the middle of the night by now. It's getting colder."

Derec nodded, folding his arms and rubbing them. "But Can Head must have reported the mugged robot to the central computer, probably right after he left us."

"As to where we are," said Ariel, "Can Head let us down through the valley floor, kind of zigzagging, and partway up the far slope. I think we're in a wheat field."

Derec reluctantly let Jeff pull him to his feet. His whole body seemed to ache. He leaned against Jeff's shoulder, breathing hard, trying to gain his balance.

127

"We woke you up because we have to keep going," said Ariel. "The Hunters aren't going to stop for the night."

"Have you got any more ideas, Derec?" Jeff asked. "Avery should have heard about the mugging by now."

Derec shook his head, still trying to wake up. "I don't know what to expect. I don't know how long that news will take to have an effect, either." He straightened up. "I meant to ask Can Head about the migration. Do you know where his assembly point is?"

"Not really," said Jeff. "He went sideways across the slope when he left, but I imagine he was heading back to that one thoroughfare they were all using."

"We don't dare try that," Derec muttered to himself.

Ariel suddenly clutched his arm. She nodded toward something over his shoulder without speaking.

Derec and Jeff turned to look. Far across the same slope, a humanoid figure was just barely distinguishable in the distance, coming toward them.

"Let's go," Derec said, feeling a faint surge of excitement. "It's not on the migration route, so it must be a Hunter, and it's sure to have seen us. I'm afraid it won't be long now."

The three of them started along the row in the opposite direction, but Derec was just barely stumbling along. As before, the others each supported one of his arms across their shoulders. Derec realized with frustration that he was now too far gone for even the adrenaline in his system to make much difference.

When they reached an intersecting row between the wheat field and a field of some low, bushy plants he could not recognize, Jeff stopped and lowered Derec's arm.

"Look, we'll have to split up." He looked back at the Hunter, which was still distant but visibly closer.

"Why bother?" Derec said wearily.

"Maybe I can divert it somehow. And if they get me first, I'm probably in the least danger from Avery. He doesn't have any business with me."

"He's crazy," Ariel said sharply. "You can't expect rational behavior from him."

"Well, maybe not. But splitting up is the best chance to keep Derec away from him a little longer. Maybe Avery will show himself in that extra time."

Derec looked up to study his face. "You sure you want to take this much risk?"

Jeff grinned at him and shrugged. "Hey, I said I owed you a favor, didn't I?"

Derec gripped his arm for a moment in thanks, then turned and started up the slope. Ariel threw her arms around Jeff in a brief hug and then hurried after Derec. Jeff moved a few meters down the slope and then got down on all fours to crawl through the low bushes of the adjacent crop field.

Derec leaned on Ariel for support as they plodded slowly up the furrow between the fields. In a moment, the tall green Auroran-bred wheat had hidden them from immediate view of the Hunter, but it would have noted the trio's movements and communicated them to the other Hunters, wherever they were.

Mandelbrot stood at the opening of one of the passes into the valley, looking out over the agricultural park. It was dimly lit and he could just barely see, with his superior robot vision, tiny figures moving in the distance. He paused to study the entire valley.

Some of the taller and thicker crops blocked his sight, but he could see a couple of humanoid robots moving straight up a row on the far slope. They were not behaving like Hunters, and he suspected that they were migrating. Down in the valley floor, he saw two large robots moving systematically among the rows of the crops and was sure that they were Hunters.

Then, at another spot on the opposite slope, he saw a human figure crawling through one of the fields. As he watched helplessly, a lone Hunter ran up behind him and lifted the human off the ground. From the lively struggle he saw he knew the human was not Derec and he judged that Ariel was smaller.

Above the struggle a short distance, he located Derec and Ariel moving painfully and slowly as they wove their way among some short trees.

Mandelbrot's programming and his understanding of the dangers posed by Dr. Avery placed Derec at the highest of his priorities. While the Hunters were programmed with a narrow definition of duty that allowed them to detain humans without harming them, Mandelbrot had a larger perspective and saw detention by the Hunters as a first step toward virtually certain harm. At the moment, he would have to ignore Jeff's capture and help Derec and Ariel if he could. He noted the positions and current movements of the Hunters he could see, and started quickly down the slope.

Derec and Ariel stumbled out of the far side of the fruit orchard onto a well-traveled footpath headed straight up and down the slope.

"I'm totally lost," Derec wheezed. He stopped, bending forward to lean on his knees. "But this must be the migration route again. Look at all the robot footprints. This valley can't have very much foot traffic. And if it did, they would have paved this."

Ariel nodded and prodded him up the slope, where the soft mud had been churned unevenly with the heavy use. The irrigation was obviously turned on at regular intervals. "C'mon," she muttered breathlessly.

They had just started up the incline when a large figure stepped out of the crops above them. It threw a massive shadow as it started down the slope toward them. Derec looked up at the great bulk of a Hunter as it moved toward them carefully, watching its precarious balance on the poor footing.

"Come on!" Ariel yanked him sideways back into the fruit orchard. "Hurry."

"I can't," he whispered apologetically. "I'm too weak to hurry." He followed her, though, until she halted abruptly a moment later.

Another Hunter was waiting for them in the trees ahead, a dark silhouette against the glow of light behind him.

They turned again and found two more Hunters pushing through the trees, breaking branches and shaking leaves as they did so, coming right up the slope without bothering to follow any rows and furrows. Their very silence and dispassionate demeanor discouraged rebellion.

Derec leaned wearily on Ariel's shoulders, unable to struggle. She wrapped her arms around him, more for his sake, he guessed, than because she was scared. He glared helplessly at the nearest Hunter.

As he watched the Hunter reaching for them he saw a weirdly flexible robot arm curl around the Hunter's neck from behind. It made a couple of quick motions and the Hunter froze, completely shut down.

Derec blinked at it, too surprised to react.

"Run!" Mandelbrot shouted, emerging from behind the Hunter. His cellular arm, which Derec had long ago installed and ordered him to disguise as a normal robotic arm of the time, was just now stiffening back to normal.

"Come on!" Ariel shoved Derec past Mandelbrot to put their protector between them and the Hunters.

They began stumbling through the trees again, their hope renewed by Mandelbrot. Ariel led him through a crooked trail, turning and twisting through the fruit trees in a clumsy, crashing route that ignored stealth entirely. At one point Derec got caught in a leafy branch and had to pause to get out. He took the moment to peer back at Mandelbrot.

Four Hunters had originally closed in on them. Mandelbrot had apparently pushed the controls on that first one to neutralize it and then had attacked the other three. By attacking them, he brought the Third Law into effect, forcing the Hunters to protect themselves. This imperative overrode even the strongest programming, so that they could not continue their pursuit until they had subdued Mandelbrot.

Mandelbrot was outnumbered, but had the advantage of instructions to use his cellular arm. Further, in the close quarters among the trees, the greater size of the Hunters impeded them. The struggle continued, buying Derec and Ariel more time as they hurried on.

Ariel led the way until finally he reached out and grabbed her, too out of breath to speak up. She waited anxiously until he could, looking around fearfully.

"Where are we going?" He panted.

"I don't know. Anywhere. Just away."

"Mandelbrot can't win that fight. He can only slow them down. Then it'll start all over again the same way."

"Have you got a better idea?" She demanded.

He nodded and got down on the ground among the trees. "I've been thinking about this park. The way that robot path is chewed up by the footprints and all. It means this park normally doesn't have an erosion problem."

"Yeah, so?"

"So these crops still need water, and it's obviously managed with their usual efficiency. If this valley is irrigated by underground pipes or something, we've had it. But I don't think the robots would do that, because leaves need external moisture, too."

"Get to the point, will you? Or let's go."

"Irrigation outlets. This valley has to have them in some form. If we turn them on, they'll eliminate our heat trail."

"Well...." She knelt down beside him. "They could be anywhere. And it's dark. Besides, Derec, this is a high-altitude valley. Maybe the natural fog and rain take care of all that."

"That would be leaving too much to chance. We have to figure this out."

"How?"

He sat back and looked at her. His legs no longer hurt; they were nearly numb. "All right. Instead of looking at random, we have to work it out logically, like the robots would. Where would you place irrigation outlets for the greatest efficiency?"

"How do I know?"

"Well, I can hardly think at all!"

"All right, all right. Concentrate. We're on a slope.... Derec, come on. This way."

He nodded and forced himself after her, stumbling on feet he could hardly feel.

After a walk that seemed much longer than it could possibly have been, they stopped along a row between the trees that ran horizontally along the slope. Now Derec was the one looking all around for Hunters that could come from any direction.

"They must use these furrows as a kind of terracing," said Ariel. "I think we're right in the middle of the vertical rows. If they put the irrigation spigots near here, they would lose the least amount to runoff down the slope. The same with fire control."

"It sounds good to me," said Derec, collapsing to the ground again. "Let's find it."

"If it's here," she added, joining him on the ground.

"I got something." Derec's hand had come across a small cylinder sticking up perhaps fifteen centimeters from the surface of the ground. He got down low to look at it in the faint light.

"Now what?" Ariel whispered, moving next to him. "It

doesn't have any controls or anything. What if the sensors are somewhere else?"

"It's possible," said Derec slowly. "But look how high it is. Why would they do that? They don't do anything sloppily here, or without a reason. They don't waste material, either."

"Derec, we can't just sit here and try to outguess them. Who knows?" She shook her head. "Maybe we should just keep running, huh?"

He shook his head. "This is the only real chance we have left. Come on, help me bury it."

"What?"

"Hurry! Why else would it be so tall? This whole thing is its own sensor. It probably judges air moisture and precipitation and who knows what."

"How do you know?"

"I think they designed it at this height so it wouldn't be covered by minor shifts in the soil during hoeing and other care. If we cover it with dirt, it'll stop sensing. Come on!" He was already scraping up the soft black soil, which the function robots seemed to keep turned constantly, and began packing it around the cylinder.

She joined him without further argument. They found the soil damp enough to stick to the cylinder if they packed it hard, and before long it was covered. Derec wiped the dirt off his hands on some leaves.

"Now what?" She asked, wiping off her own hands. "Nothing's happening."

CHAPTER 18
DOWN A HOLE

At the far end of the valley, Wolruf sat quivering in the chilly air. She was huddled high in the mountains in a vertical crevice of rock. This was the compromise she had reached for her conundrum: she was in the valley where she could try to observe the humans or even Mandelbrot if they were here when day broke. At the same time, she would not lead the Hunters following her directly to them.

Now she could not see any of them in the faint light down in the valley. In the nearer regions below her, function robots were visible doing their regular chores among the crops. Her physiology kept her just warm enough at this altitude to remain for a while, but she was not comfortable. Nor did she have the energy left to run farther.

She waited patiently, reviewing the moves she had made to break her trail. None of them could avoid a systematic search by the Hunters if they were close enough to detect her heat. Also, the Hunters probably had checked the pass at some point, because it was a bottleneck that could quickly tell them if she was inside the valley or out.

If her heat trail had faded before they had reached it, they still had physical signs to rely on. She had been as careful as possible, but the robotic vision of the Hunters could detect extreme detail. The rest was up to them.

Her ears perked up at the sound of footsteps on the rock fall below her. With no more energy left for fleeing, she waited patiently. The giant shape of a Hunter emerged from the darkness, thrown into silhouette by the distant glow emanating from the crops below. She knew it would not harm her, but it would take her prisoner and possibly deliver her to Dr. Avery, who could certainly harm her if he wished. She shivered as the Hunter reached down to pick her up.

Derec was staring disconsolately at the dirt-covered sensor when it suddenly erupted in an uneven spray, knocking loose some of the dirt. Ariel and he both flinched. All around them, other spigots were also spraying jets of fine mist into the air.

"That's it!" Derec lifted his arms toward her. "Let's go. Can you help me up?"

Ariel took his arms and pulled. His legs gave out under him. She wasn't strong enough to lift him.

She started to pull again.

"I can't walk any more." His lower legs and feet had lost all feeling.

"You can't walk at all?" Her shoulders slumped.

"But I can crawl. Let's go."

"Derec . . . ?"

"Come on!" He started crawling through the soft earth, which was quickly turning to mud.

She stood and walked alongside him. "This is crazy. We're hardly getting anywhere."

"We have a lot more time now. The Hunters can't follow our heat trail so they'll have to start a pattern search. And at least one of them will have to carry Mandelbrot after they've shut him down."

"Derec, you've only gone two meters!"

He stopped, sighing, and looked ahead. She was right. He could barely move. "Hey—what's that thing?"

"What?" She looked, too.

Some kind of large rectangular shape, at least a cubic meter in size, was emerging from the ground below the trees.

"That . . . thing, there. We haven't seen one of those before." He started crawling again.

"There's one behind us, too," she said. "And beyond that

one. They're coming up all over. They were completely hidden before."

"We must have triggered them along with the irrigation. Go see what it is."

She hurried ahead and stopped in front of the object, bending low in front of it. After a moment, she came back and knelt down. "I think we can get inside it. It looks like a ventilation duct or something."

Derec nodded. He had stopped crawling to get his breath again. His head was spinning dizzily.

When he got down on all fours and moved under him, he let her. She gathered his arms around her neck and maneuvered under him. Then, supporting his weight, she began to crawl much faster than he had, carrying as much of his weight as she could.

He hung on with his arms and closed his eyes against the spray of water.

"Here," she said, after a few moments.

He opened his eyes into a gaping black opening with no other features. As she eased out from under him, he reached inside and felt for the shape of the object.

"It's not a straight drop." She helped him climb inside. "You can feel a gradual incline."

Derec hesitated, too disoriented to speak but still reluctant to throw himself into an unknown hole.

"Go on, get in before the Hunters see us."

He was losing all sense of his surroundings. Following directions was easier than arguing. He worked his way inside the opening and then suddenly was sliding downward and accelerating.

All was in darkness. He felt a rushing of air, the smooth pressure of the surface against his back as he slid, and Ariel bumping against him from above as she slid with him. Vaguely, he realized he was too exhausted to feel any fear.

He should have been terrified of winding up in a moving fan blade, for instance, or in the workings of some mysterious robot creation that would convert them both to fertilizer. Apparently he had been on Robot City too long for that. The robots couldn't allow that much danger to a human to exist here.

No, that wasn't it, either. The reason was even simpler. Nothing on this planet was more frightening than the chemfets destroying his body from the inside at this very moment.

The sensation of falling continued as they entered some turns, gradual curves, and finally reached a sudden upturn.

In the short ascent, gravity broke their momentum and then they slid backward again. Derec lay motionless, aware that they had stopped in the bottom of this thing, whatever it was. No light reached them at all.

He felt Ariel move a little, probably getting her bearings.

"Derec?" She said softly. "Are you hurt?"

A moment passed before he had the breath to answer. "No," he whispered. "But I've had it."

"We're safe now," she said, feeling for him and stroking his hair. "At least from the Hunters. I'm sure of it. They'll have to search the entire valley, and every one of these things. And these were popping up every few meters, it looked like. . . . well, every fifty or sixty, anyhow. Without a heat trail to follow, it'll take them forever."

"I can't do it."

"But we're onto him! Avery, I mean. I'm sure of it." She shuffled around and seemed to stand. "You know that upward curve at the end of our . . . little ride? It's here and not very high. The duct continues on a level from here. Say, you know what else? There are handholds of some kind on the side opposite the one we slid down."

"Maybe for service robots to make repairs down here." He thought a moment. The temptation to go on was strong. Confronting the crazy doctor after all the suffering he had endured . . . but he couldn't move. All he wanted to do was sleep.

"I think you're right," he said finally. "This is a ventilation duct. From the size and number of them, it must lead to an immense living space."

"Avery's home. Robots wouldn't need it or the produce in the valley. Come on, let's go. I'll help you up."

"You'll have to go on alone. I honestly can't move."

She was quiet a moment. "Do you really want me to go on without you?"

"Yes."

"All right," she said slowly. She waited, perhaps trying to think of something else to say. Then she got her arms around him and embraced him very hard, and held on.

He was too weak to respond. After a moment, he felt her let go and stand up. Then she was climbing, and he heard her moving down the ventilation duct away from him.

He closed his eyes and slept.

Ariel felt her way forward slowly with her hands as she crawled, not making any move until she knew what was ahead of her. She was still in absolute darkness in some kind of giant tube that was so far stretching straight ahead on a level course. With Derec unable to move, she was painfully aware that she was the last of their group to have a chance at finding Dr. Avery.

She was not exactly in top condition herself. Her hands and feet were painfully cold and she was drenched from the sprinklers. She was worn out, too, though not sick like Derec was. The climb up the mountainside and down into the valley had taken a lot of energy out of her.

She hoped, with guarded optimism, that her memory was growing stronger. Those weird memory fugues had grown less frequent and she wished fervently that none would strike while she was alone in this thing, whatever it was.

She began to find branches and intersections in the passageway. Without any way to pick one direction over another, she attempted to go as straight as she could. Going in roughly one direction would at least prevent her from wandering hopelessly in circles. She suspected that the intersecting tunnels represented those other openings on the surface they had seen.

After a while, she thought she had picked out a pattern. From what she could feel, smaller tunnels seemed to converge more often and become larger ones consistently to her left. She began to move leftward and discovered that the tunnels were now high enough for her to stand if she bent over.

Now that she was moving in this direction, more tunnels converged around her all the time. Then they started branching out again, some of them splitting off above her. Finally she realized that she could see hints of shapes: dark spaces that represented openings one way, a faint reflection of an inner surface another way.

The traces of a light source shone from just one direction.

She dropped to all fours again to pursue the light source, now more concerned with making noise than with the height of the tunnel.

Around a curve, she reached something recognizable: a covered opening into a room. Barely daring to breathe, she moved as quietly as she could toward it until she could peek through the opening.

It was nearly opaque.

The room was lit, but she couldn't see much. It was carpeted in brown. Nor could she hear anything.

After the silence had continued, she decided that she would have to risk entering the room. She began studying the edge of the covering to see if she could get it loose. In a moment, she found that pressure on the covering itself caused a hole to appear in the middle. The substance, whatever it was, receded from the hole to fade outward into the surrounding wall until the vent was entirely open.

She let out a sigh of relief that the room was deserted. It was still silent, as well. After shifting around to get her feet out first, she dropped to the floor of the room and looked around.

It was a small room, perhaps only three meters cubed. The brown carpeting went all the way up the walls and covered the ceiling as well. The light came from a globe floating just under the center of the ceiling.

She looked again at the ceiling, then at the walls. The room was not built on right angles. The corners were slightly askew.

A couple of computer tapes were piled on the floor. In one corner, a small stuffed animal of unrecognizable type lay on its side. The room was not being used for anything that she could see.

This was not what Ariel had expected from Dr. Avery.

The door was closed. She held her breath and pushed the stud on the wall next to it. It slid open silently.

She remained where she was, waiting. When nothing happened, she stuck her head out slowly. She found a hallway extending maybe six meters one way and four the other. The hallway itself was oddly shaped, but familiar—then she recognized it. It was a hollow three-dimensional rendition of the Key to Perihelion.

She stepped into the hallway. The closed doors at each end of it were also shaped like the Keys. She chose one and walked toward it.

This one opened as she reached it. She hesitated, then edged through. Her mouth dropped open in surprise.

This room reminded her of some ancient historical paintings she had seen. The high vaulted ceiling was at least two stories high and hung with curtains of burgundy velvet. Imitation Renaissance paintings in garish gold frames seemed to fit what she remembered of that period . . . or did they? Yet that furniture . . . was classic Auroran design, developed many centuries later. She looked up again, trying to orient herself . . . and shuffled quickly to one side to catch her balance.

This room was also askew. Worse than that, she guessed, it was not built on angles at all. Though the corners of the ceiling and walls were partly hidden by curtains, the whole room seemed oddly rounded, even twisted out of shape, as though the room had begun as a rectangle, had started to melt, and then had frozen again.

She started across the room to look more closely at the furniture. After four steps, the floor gave out beneath her and she fell, sliding this time down a short, twisting chute. She heard the trapdoor above her hiss closed again as she landed somewhere else with a thump.

This room was tiny, with just barely enough room for her to stand up. It, too, was in the shape of the Keys. There was a door in each wall that was big enough, and nothing else. The walls glowed with light, as in the Compass Tower. She pressed a stud by one of the doors.

The door slid open to reveal a solid glowing wall. She opened another one. This door opened to reveal a dark, narrow hallway. Before trying it, she pushed another stud.

A weirdly sculptured face stared at her from an archaic red brick wall. It had pointed ears, a long pointed face, and was laughing. Grimacing, she closed that one and tried another.

Another dark hallway stretched in front of her.

She had to go somewhere. With a glance at the other open doorway, she edged inside. The walls here didn't glow, and she slid her feet carefully along the floor before committing her weight forward. After a few steps, the corridor began to curve.

A moment later, she had followed it right back to the same little room again.

CHAPTER 19
THE CORPSE

Ariel closed the doors to the circular hallway and stood inside the room. It might not have an exit, of course; this was the work of a paranoid whose tendencies had been openly revealed. The room could just be a prison.

"Well, now what?" She said aloud.

A muffled response sounded behind one of the doors. She pressed the stud and found herself looking at the grotesque sculptured face again. All its features were exaggerated.

"What did you say?" She demanded.

"Pull my nose," it said.

"Who are you?"

"Pull my nose."

"What happens when I do?"

"Pull my nose."

"Is that all you can say?"

"Pull my nose."

She watched it for a moment. "One, two, three."

"Pull my nose."

She figured it out, then. This was a function robot without a positronic brain. It had one line to say, triggered by any sound of human speech.

Holding her breath, she pulled its nose.

The long, narrow nose stretched toward her and then suddenly snapped back, out of her grasp. On impact, the entire sculpture collapsed into itself, inverted, and pushed itself out the other way. Then the brick wall broke into quarters and each piece receded sideways, carrying the inverted face with it.

She was looking down a short ramp into another corridor, this one lined with glowing stones cut in the shape of the Keys but not in a smooth surface. Their corners protruded irregularly out of the wall to create a jagged, textured wall. The entire shape of the corridor as she faced the opening was in the shape of the Keys, as well.

Still stepping carefully, she ventured down the ramp. After a moment, she realized that she was chillier than before . . . air was moving against her soaked clothing. Puzzled, she turned around—and found the walls, ceiling, and floor behind her converging to pinch off the corridor after she had passed.

She hurried forward a little, despite her caution, and came up against a stone wall at the end. Starting to panic, she ran her hands across the stones, feeling for a control of some kind. She felt nothing and whirled around to look at the shrinking corridor.

Suddenly something dropped from the ceiling in front of her and she flattened against the end wall, trying to see the object as it swayed before her face. She recognized it as Wolruf's head, dangling on a long piece of rope tied into an ancient noose.

As she stared at it in horror, she realized that it was only a function robot rendered in realistic detail.

"Why arr 'u 'err?" The robot asked, in Wolruf's voice.

Ariel's spine prickled at the sound. She glanced behind the hanging head. The corridor had stopped closing behind her and now had left her in a very small dungeonlike space.

"Wrong answer," said the robot, though she hadn't spoken.

Suddenly the floor rose under Ariel's feet, pushing her up toward the ceiling. The rope retracted with her, keeping the Wolruf head level with her as she rose. The ceiling opened and then the section of floor stopped, now flush with the floor just above the stone corridor.

The abrupt halt threw her off balance and she fell on a rich, gold carpet. Above her, five elaborate chandeliers sparkled and shone from a surprisingly low beamed ceiling. She rose up on her elbows, looking around fearfully.

She was in a library. Shelves of antique books, not computer tapes, stretched around all the walls and were protected by a transparent barrier of some kind. Turning, she stepped off the lift platform away from the Wolruf head.

A candelabra of some sort was on a shelf outside the transparent barrier that protected the books. It stood inside a blue and white bowl, leaning to one side. The candelabra was on a round base, with one central stem holding one candle and four branches arching upward on each side to total nine. She had never seen one before, whatever it was, and thought it seemed out of place here, as though someone had set it down and forgotten it.

She stepped back and looked at the bowl. It was large enough to serve four or five people plenty of food. Light blue designs danced around the white background on the outside. It had never been meant to hold a candelabra, though. Someone had left these here carelessly.

"What iss it?" The Wolruf head asked.

Ariel flinched at the sound and looked at the head. "A candleholder of some kind, obviously."

"Wrong again."

One of the shelved walls glided away soundlessly. She stood where she was, eyeing the dark opening that appeared. An animal—no, a function robot, almost certainly—stepped into a space where light fell on it. It had Wolruf's caninoid body and Ariel's own face.

"If you're standing on the surface of the planet Earth in Webster Groves, Missouri," said the robot-Ariel, "which way is Robot City?"

She stared at it hopelessly. "I'm no navigator. Not without some kind of information to use, anyway."

Robot-Ariel cocked her head, turned, and trotted away.

The wall of shelves slid back into place.

Ariel sank to the floor in a mixture of relief and despair. She couldn't just go on wandering aimlessly in the real-life manifestation of one man's insanity. If this place offered a way out, she could figure it out. If it didn't, she might as well stay in this room instead of going forward into some dungeon cell or something worse.

As before, her knowledge of Dr. Avery was the only source

of clues she had, and she no longer had Jeff's memories or Derec's facility with robots to help. All right. Basically, what did she know?

She knew he was a genius, that he was paranoid, that he wanted to create a perfect society. But what did this crazy place have to do with order and rationality?

What was it doing on Robot City?

Everything she knew about Robot City said that this place just didn't belong here at all. The more she thought about it, the more she realized that every line of thought brought her back to that one conclusion. "That's it," she whispered to herself suddenly. "He's gone over the edge. He's even crazier than before."

In the heart of a planet-wide city based on logic and efficiency, its creator had lost his mind.

She smiled at the irony. It wasn't funny, exactly, but it was . . . funny. Somehow.

Exhaustion and fear made her giddy. She began to giggle. The more she thought about this—about all their discussions of the Laws of Robotics and all their convoluted efforts to reason with the positronic brains of the robots—and how it had led to *this*. . . . She really began to laugh. She fell onto the floor on her back, laughing in the little room by herself.

The wall of shelves slid open again, apparently triggered by the sound of her laughter.

Suddenly on guard again, she sat up and looked around. The function robot with her face was back.

"If you're standing on the surface of the planet Earth in Webster Groves, Missouri," said the robot-Ariel again, "which way is Robot City?"

Ariel giggled again. "Up, of course." She laughed—and the floor gave way beneath her.

She was in one more chute, twisting in a tight downward spiral. Just as it began to level off, the dark space ahead of her irised open into light. She spilled out onto a polished hardwood floor.

Shaken by the ride, she lay still for a moment gazing at a very high beamed ceiling that was nearly lost in shadows. She turned her head to the side and found walls of gray stone, precisely chiseled and fit again in the modular shape of the Key to

Perihelion. The room was huge, stretching meters on each side of her.

She raised onto her elbow, still getting her bearings. The end of a large, intricately carved table was in front of her. Its legs and feet were sculpted in the shape of some furry, clawed animal she did not recognize. It was made of a dark, deeply polished wood.

Struggling to rise, she reached up and grabbed the edge of the table. She pulled herself up to lean on it and then froze in surprise. At the far end of the table, many meters away, a man sat in a high, straight-backed chair with a gigantic fire blazing behind him in a stone fireplace twice her height.

"Welcome, Ariel. I am Dr. Avery."

She stared at him with nothing to say. After all the effort to find him, landing here like this was so unexpected that she hadn't formed any plan of attack, any arguments to use with him. She wasn't ready to talk to him.

"You are welcome to warm yourself by the fire," said her host.

She was willing to stay chilly to keep away from him, but she wanted to stall a little if she could, without getting too close. Slowly, she moved around the corner of the table and began to walk down the side of it. Dr. Avery seemed relaxed, even unconcerned, as he fingered some small object in front of him on the table.

The long, narrow table had all kinds of articles on it: flowers, dishes, trinkets, small sculptures. She didn't dare take the time to look. Her eyes remained on Dr. Avery.

He was short, looking especially so in the high-backed chair. His build was stocky. Wavy white hair framed his face, which was also adorned with a bushy mustache. He looked friendly and benign.

His coat was too big, as she remembered from the other times she had seen him, and he still wore a white shirt with a ruffled collar.

He didn't look crazy.

Ariel stopped a good four meters away, still watching him. What was a crazy man supposed to look like?

"I was not expecting visitors, Ariel," said Dr. Avery. He was still studying the object in front of him. "Though I had warning that oddities, shall we say, were occurring in this vicinity."

He didn't sound crazy, either.

"Ariel, you don't remember me, do you?" His gaze remained on the table.

"Yes," she said timidly.

"No, not really. You remember me after the performance of *Hamlet* and when the Hunter robots located all of you in the passageways beneath the city and you remember me from when they brought you to me. That's all."

"That's when we met."

He smiled and picked up the little object. "Automatic alarms were triggered tonight. A couple of them, in fact. When a man who enjoys his privacy feels it may be disturbed, he likes to have alarms installed. Did you trigger them, Ariel?"

She watched him silently, surprised by his changing subjects so quickly.

"A humanoid robot mysteriously shut down completely just a short distance from here. Then a shift in the soil was reported. Did you do those, Ariel?"

"Kind of. I guess."

"You guess. I guess, too. Violations of the provisional Laws of Humanics? Perhaps. I haven't yet investigated the details. But how did you enter my abode?"

Derec was lying helpless along her route. She didn't dare answer that question.

"One of the few weaknesses in my security here is in my emergency ventilation system. It opens when unexplained malfunctions occur in this valley." He sighed. "I could have had the robots make it entry-proof, but it happens to represent my escape routes, as well. If no one could get in that way, then I couldn't get out that way, could I?"

"What do you want?" she demanded, hoping to get him off that subject. "What is all this about, anyway?"

"Of course, I do have a maze that one must negotiate. It acts as a buffer zone. Perhaps you managed that."

She was shaking with tension, unable to get a handle on a conversation that kept jumping topics.

"By the way, I've misplaced a couple of items. Have you seen them? One is an antique menorah crafted in the ancient Earth empire of the czars. The other is a Ming Dynasty bowl."

She stared at him, vaguely remembering a fancy bowl.

"You really don't remember me, do you, Ariel?"

"Why do you keep saying that?"

"You have new memories now, clearly. You are not the Ariel I last saw. You are again the real Ariel, if you only knew it. A few more accurate memories will trigger the rest, I believe."

"What are you talking about?"

"Your memories now are accurate. It is the real you. The one you thought was you . . . no. You never knew a Spacer who contaminated you. You never had a disease. You will, I sadly suppose, recall the name . . . David Avery." For the first time, then, he looked up and met her eyes.

David Avery. David. Derec . . . ?

Suddenly memories did come flooding back. "David! Derec is David! And you hated me!"

"Oh, now, now. What I attempted with you failed. Bygones are bygones, eh?"

"You . . . what have you done?" She was horrified, yet fascinated. Finally, after such a long time, the mysteries were being answered. "Oh, no. Wait a minute. Is Derec really David . . . or what about the corpse? Was that David? Did you kill him?" She was nearly hysterical, partly from the shock of understanding.

"No, no, of course not." He waved a hand in dismissal. "The corpse, as you call it, was merely a synthetic physical imitation of David. A good one, of course, that used genuine human blood. I used him in a dry-run test of David's encounter with Robot City."

Ariel, still quivering with tension but now composed again, leaned against the table for support. "So you planted memory chemfets and disease in me a long time ago to give me a false memory. Memories of events that never existed to replace my memories of real life. And . . . Derec is David."

"And you were his lover. Oh, by the way, didn't you ever wonder what happened to the corpse? The cleaning robots recognized it as nothing more than waste material and hauled it away."

"You destroyed my memory," she said again, slowly. "And his. The amnemonic plague was artificial, created by chemfets. It was you. To separate David and me. You must have given him his amnesia for the same reason."

"I always knew you had intelligence. My son's taste was always exceptional."

"And ever since my memory returned on Earth, I withheld telling Derec the truth because I was afraid these memories might not be correct. All this time, I could have put his mind at ease if I had only trusted my memories."

"A compliment. Consider my actions a compliment. Breaking your hold on my son's will required extreme measures. Judge it as the extent to which he cares about you." He leaned back in his chair, holding the little item he had been playing with. "Cared, I should say. He doesn't remember even now, of course . . . but he does seem to have formed an affection for you all over again, seen by the way you two have remained a team."

"You practically destroyed two people just to keep them apart." Her anger was mixed with sheer astonishment.

"Ah, no. Sorry. You are not so important as you think. My other motive was to test my son's resourcefulness. You see, if he succeeded in manipulating and controlling Robot City, then he was truly worthy of my final plan for him."

"Final plan . . . ? Do you mean to say," she said slowly, "that you wiped his memory and placed him on that asteroid as a *test?*"

"It is what I mean to say and what I have said." He sat up and for the first time his face reflected enthusiasm. "You see, Robot City has been finished. Now each of the humanoid robots here has had implanted in his body . . . one or two duplicate Keys to Perihelion. Even now, they are marching to predetermined sites around this planet from which they will launch themselves to different galaxies. In each galaxy, they will begin replication of themselves and construction of more Robot Cities. And David, my son who has now earned the right to act as my son, will control each and every robot in every Robot City . . . making him the most powerful man in the universe!"

"He *what? How?*"

"The chemfets, my dear. The memory chemfets in his body. You see, a tiny Robot City is growing inside him . . . and when it matures, his mere thoughts will control every Avery robot in the universe."

"Oh, no . . . you *are* insane. You don't know what's happened to him!"

"Of course I do. The chemfets develop slowly and cause certain physical disabilities. I know that. They behave like a disease and can even cause the formation of antibodies in the bloodstream."

"You're murdering him! He's almost dead now!"

"Oh, nonsense. The chemfets didn't kill you, did they? I wouldn't kill him, would I? After all this? Why would I throw away all this effort?"

"But you're wrong! Your chemfets for me were much simpler. He's *dying!*"

"Where is he?"

She paused, suddenly realizing the dilemma that Derec and she had never solved. They could not force Dr. Avery to cooperate. He had to be convinced.

"The central computer is calling. For several moments now, I have ignored a little light on my table here. I have done so because I know what it signifies, I believe. Excuse me, will you?"

Ariel stared at him, amazed at his composure and his refusal to believe her.

A small section of the table in front of Dr. Avery swiveled to reveal a computer console on what had been the underside of the table. "Would you like to hear?" He pushed a button. "I'll set it on voice, which I usually find intrusive. Report," he said into the console.

"HUNTERS REPORT APPREHENSION OF HUMAN NAMED DEREC."

"Thought so," said Dr. Avery pleasantly. "Report status of Hunter project."

"THE FOLLOWING HAVE BEEN APPREHENDED AND ARE HELD ON THE NORTH SLOPE OF THE VALLEY: DEREC, JEFF LEONG, MANDELBROT, WOLRUF. STILL MISSING: ARIEL WELSH."

Dr. Avery laughed casually. "Now, who would have thought I could outperform my own team of Hunter robots?"

Ariel's heart was pounding with tension. If Derec was already in Avery's control, very little risk was left. "Dr. Avery. Will you agree to a test?"

"Eh? What kind of test? Haven't we had enough testing around here for a while?"

"Have the robots check David and see if he is in danger from the chemfets. They'll tell you."

"A party," said Dr. Avery. "An excellent idea. I'll have the Hunters bring everyone. We'll have a party." He tossed the object in his hand over his shoulder into the fire.

Ariel saw it clearly for the first time. It was a small model of a humanoid robot.

CHAPTER 20
TO RULE IN ROBOT CITY

Ariel watched the gray stones, or whatever they were, in the wall dissolve into air for a moment and the Hunters brought in their captives through the opening. The first one carried Derec gently in his arms as though he were a giant baby, but limp and unconscious. The second entered holding Jeff Leong firmly by one upper arm as they walked. The third held Wolruf cradled on one elbow and the fourth marched in with Mandelbrot lying over his shoulder, completely shut down.

The stone wall reformed behind them.

"Clear the table," said Dr. Avery. "Don't worry about where the stuff goes."

The Hunter carrying Mandelbrot laid him down on the floor and then extended his arm along the full width of the table at the far end. He then walked down the length of the table as his arm knocked everything it struck onto the floor. By the time he had reached the near end, Dr. Avery had himself swept aside the items within his own reach.

Ariel watched in horror. She had never seen a humanoid robot act so messily, even destructively, on a casual instruction. This one must have known that Dr. Avery wanted to be taken literally and did not want him to remove the items on the table with any care.

"Put him down." Dr. Avery nodded to the Hunter holding Derec. Then he waved at the one carrying Mandelbrot. "And turn him on, will you? This won't be much of a party with so many people feeling unsociable."

Ariel felt some relief as the Hunter located Mandelbrot's controls and activated him again. "Mandelbrot, tell him. Tell Dr. Avery what's happening to Derec."

Mandelbrot scanned the room quickly. His observation probably told him as much about the current situation as Ariel already knew. "Dr. Avery," he said clearly. "Derec has undergone extreme physical debilitation that continues to increase. He believes that the chemfets you placed in his body are killing him. My observation of his symptoms confirms that likelihood."

"Doesn't anybody here want to have a party?" Dr. Avery sighed. "Everyone is so morbid. Say, Mr. Leong. Haven't we met before? Not lately and not on this planet, however."

"That's right," Jeff said sullenly. "You were more sociable in those days, yourself."

Dr. Avery pushed back his chair and stood up. Trailing the fingers of one hand along the table, he walked down its length looking at the motionless figure of Derec. "He has done very well. I have not given him any challenge he cannot surmount."

"Till *now,*" Ariel insisted. "How can you take a risk like this? Even your own robots wouldn't risk his life for a test."

Jeff, Wolruf, and Mandelbrot all looked at her in surprise.

"Oh, I don't think he'll have any trouble. He'll be fine." Dr. Avery nodded to himself.

"Aren't you even going to test him? Check him out in your laboratory?" She cried.

"He'll be fine. Let's have a party." Dr. Avery turned to the Hunter who had brought Derec in. "Take him to one of the guest rooms, though. We can't have a party with a guest lying motionless on the dining table, can we?"

"Hold it!" Ariel got between Derec and that Hunter. "Can't you understand that he's dying?"

"Pick him up," Dr. Avery ordered.

The Hunter gently but firmly moved Ariel aside and lifted Derec. She threw her arms around Derec's shoulders and hung on. "Wait! Mandelbrot, they're letting him die!"

Mandelbrot was standing by the Hunter who had brought him in. That Hunter, however, had one hand resting on Mandelbrot's open control panel. At the slightest resistance from Mandelbrot, the Hunter would shut him down again.

The next sequence of events took place very quickly, some of it timed by the speed of positronic brains.

Suddenly Jeff, who was still held by one Hunter, reached over and started grabbing Mandelbrot's Hunter by the neck, feeling around quickly for his controls. The Hunter, required by the Third Law to protect himself, grasped Jeff's arm in his other hand. In the tiny fraction of a second that the Third Law imperative was foremost in the Hunter's mind, Mandelbrot stepped away and closed his own control panel with his flexible cellular arm.

From the moment Mandelbrot was free, the battle was on. His belief that Derec's life was in danger forced him under the First Law to take Ariel's anxiety seriously. At the same time, the Hunters believed Dr. Avery's declaration that Derec was not in danger, so under the Second Law they followed their orders from him to detain and control the others.

Mandelbrot also shot out an array of information through his comlink to the Hunters. He told them of Derec's delicate condition, of Ariel's memory failures, of their physical hardships. In the tiny instant it required, he demanded that they back away from Derec and Ariel immediately or risk major violations of the First Law.

He did not know if it would work, but even the slightest hesitation and doubt on their part would help.

Even as Mandelbrot sent these signals, he moved toward Derec. Ariel let go of Derec to grab the Hunter holding him, knowing that the Hunter would be impeded by the necessity of not harming Derec or her. In a couple of quick moves, Mandelbrot's flexible arm had shut down this Hunter in a motionless standing position, still holding Derec. Mandelbrot and Ariel lifted Derec and placed him back on the table.

One Hunter had now taken Wolruf and Jeff under each arm and had lifted them into the air where they squirmed helplessly.

"You're hurting me!" Jeff shouted. "First Law violation!"

The Hunter was not convinced.

"Stop them!" Dr. Avery screamed. "Don't hurt them, but stop them! And don't collide with David! His condition is too fragile!"

"You've got to believe us!" Ariel shouted, turning to plead with him. "You don't want him hurt, either! Just test him!"

They stood face-to-face now and Ariel saw a strangely twisted expression on his face. It was an angry smile of triumph. For the first time since meeting him, she understood that he truly was crazy—and beyond persuasion by reason.

"You did this!" Dr. Avery hissed in her face. "Without you, these extremes would not have been necessary. Leave him alone!"

"How *dare* you blame this on me?" She screamed, and in a mixture of frustration, rage, and exhaustion she lost her temper completely. Unbound by any Laws except her conscience, she launched herself at him angrily, grabbing his sideburns in both hands.

One of the four Hunters had been shut down. Another was holding Jeff and Wolruf away from Mandelbrot. Mandelbrot was trying to reach the unguarded control panel of this one with his flexible arm while using his other arm to grapple with the other two Hunters. With all the robots' attention focused on each other across the room, they did not notice or respond to the potential harm Ariel and Dr. Avery might do to each other.

Dr. Avery grimaced in pain and growled at her as they shuffled around in a tight struggle.

Deep in the darkness of Derec's mind, robots marched. He was lying on his back in darkness as robots stepped in rhythmic time with a precision only robots could maintain. They strode by him in files that split at his feet and tramped past him on either side, their heavy feet pounding by his head. He was ignored, insignificant, not even present in their positronic awareness.

Out of darkness, the robots marched. A slight glow of skyline shone behind them but mostly he could see only a blood-red sky above, one that had never really existed, where space stretched endlessly beyond the planet. Still the robots streamed past, intent on their destination with that single-mindedness so evident in the Avery creations.

Avery. Avery. Avery. The beat of pounding feet seemed to take on the name. It was name of his enemy, the name of . . . of . . .

His dream shifted. Even as the robots continued to march, he watched strange green shapes, some cubic and some pyramidal, rising in the air around him. When he reached for them, missing, he floated up after them. They turned, light shining off their different facets as they rose. He snagged one and it became a computer console under his hands.

He was floating higher in the air now. The blood night of Robot City threw its myriad streets into a golden glow without logic or explanation, and still the robots marched. His fingers seemed to type without thought from his mind: "Stop them."

"NO," answered the central computer.

"Stop the city."

"NO."

"Why not?"

"WHO ARE YOU?"

"I am I am I am . . . who am I?"

"WHERE ARE YOU?"

"I am . . . Robot City."

"ERROR. I AM ROBOT CITY," said the central computer. "WHO ARE YOU?"

"Who am I?"

"YOU ARE DAVID AVERY."

"I am David Avery?" Derec stared at the name on the dream console. The dream console was green, made of a floating pyramid like a tiny Compass Tower . . . made of a chemfet.

He looked around. This wasn't the real central computer. The blood-red sky told him how small he was. He was floating in his own bloodstream, watching chemfets and Robot City grow inside him . . .

"I am David Avery," he typed. "I am David Avery. This is my bloodstream, my body, my . . . Robot City."

"ACKNOWLEDGED," said the central computer.

The robots stopped marching. He floated in the air high above them now and looked down on the endless rows of robots. Every single Avery robot on the planet raised its head to await Derec's commands.

He raised his head and shouted, "Robot City is mine! I am David Avery and I am Robot City!"

At his shout, the sky split. The scene dissipated. He blinked and gradually heard more yells and scraping sounds around him. A chandelier was blazing over him. He took in a deep breath—and realized that, for the first time in a very long time, his body felt normal.

His mind was clearing slowly as he came awake. His body was tired, and cold with dampness, but the weird stiffness was gone. He was no longer in physical danger.

"Derec!" Ariel yelled. "You're awake? Tell him! Tell Avery what's happening to you."

Avery? With a surge of fear and anger, Derec sat up and found himself on a long table. He turned. Ariel and—his father, Dr. Avery, were scuffling around in a circle.

"I'm all right," Derec said hoarsely.

"What?" Ariel looked at him in surprise. "Then help me!"

"No!" Dr. Avery roared. "No! This is not right! You must help me!"

"Help you?" Derec shouted angrily. "You're crazy!"

"Kill them!" Dr. Avery screamed at the Hunters. "Kill them! You must kill them or everything will be for naught!"

Ariel pulled free of him and turned toward the two Hunters who were still functioning; Mandelbrot had succeeded in shutting down a second one. "Dr. Avery is mad. You understand? He's . . . he's malfunctioned. You remember the Laws of Humanics that the Supervisors were trying to devise?"

Dr. Avery had backed away toward the fireplace. "You must save us!" he shouted at the Hunters. "Kill them!"

"Listen to him," Ariel called out, now more in control. "His orders violate the First Law. You can't trust his orders any more. Orders that violate the Laws of Robotics also violate the Second Law of Humanics, which says humans will not give robots unreasonable orders. Listen to him, and you'll understand that he can't be followed anymore." If the Hunters had learned how she and Jeff and Derec had shut down Pei, they wouldn't listen to her, either.

The remaining Hunters had not moved. One held Jeff and Wolruf. The other was in a stand-off with Mandelbrot, as each tried to reach the manual controls of the other to shut him down.

"Acknowledged," said the Hunter holding Jeff and Wolruf. "Dr. Avery's instructions cannot be followed. However, the central computer also directs us. We are still under orders to detain the members of your group without harming them."

Dr. Avery had cowered into a corner, still shouting.

"I am Robot City now," said Derec. "The chemfets in my body have matured and I have reprogrammed them." He visualized the computer console in his mind. Maybe he wouldn't always have to do that, but right now it made the task easier. "Central computer," he thought. "Eliminate the orders to the Hunter robots regarding Derec or David Avery, Ariel Welsh, the robot Mandelbrot, and the caninoid alien Wolruf. Then notify all pertinent robots of the change." Then aloud he said, "Hunters. A new order should come through to you—"

"Acknowledged," said the Hunter in front of Mandelbrot. He straightened, dropping his guard.

"Acknowledged," echoed the other Hunter, releasing Jeff and Wolruf.

"I received it also," said Mandelbrot.

"Now, then," said Derec, turning to Dr. Avery.

Dr. Avery was standing in the corner of the room to one side of the giant fireplace. As the others turned to watch him, he drew himself up. "Consider what you have accomplished, my son," he said. "Think of it. Everything I envisioned to this point has come to pass as I intended. Well, almost—never mind this young woman. You rule in Robot City. Soon you will rule in every Robot City, in thousands of them throughout all the galaxies."

A stinging sadness came over Derec, draining his anger. "You're . . . not right. Not right in the head. You started out seeking a utopia and instead you've gotten sidetracked. This has become a springboard for power, not for good. Maybe if you took it easy for a while, got some professional advice . . ."

"You dare to order *me?*" Dr. Avery yelled. "No! You join me! I order it!"

"I'm not a robot. You can't order me." Derec turned to the Hunters. "Please detain my . . . detain Dr. Avery without harming him."

The two Hunters started forward.

With a twisted sneer, Dr. Avery lifted a small object in one hand: a Key to Perihelion. He laughed derisively and then vanished.

Derec walked slowly to the head of the table, still looking at the space where Dr. Avery had stood. His relief was tinged with melancholy at understanding his father's condition.

Everyone was watching him.

He turned at his father's chair, resting one hand on the back of it. "Mandelbrot, please put those items on the floor back on the table. Hunters, your task is over. Please return to your holding area, or wherever you normally reside."

The robots obeyed.

"Are you really okay?" Ariel asked, moving toward him. "David?"

He grinned and put his arm around her. "I guess so. David seems to be okay, and so is Derec."

"I seem to be okay, too." She put her arms around him and they embraced.

None of them wanted to split up for the night or go exploring for bedrooms in the Avery estate. As tired as they were, Derec, Ariel, Jeff, and Wolruf were able to sleep by the fire even on the hard floor. Derec knew that Dr. Avery might have transported elsewhere on the planet and could still pose a danger, but he doubted any threat would be immediate. Just before going to sleep, he gave a general order throughout Robot City that all robots were to remain where they were until further notice, except for minimal activities to keep the city operating. That way he would have time later to figure out exactly what status the city was in and how to return the robots from their assembly points to normal duties. With Mandelbrot standing by and Robot City under his own mental control, he fell into a genuine sleep.

The next morning, Ariel pointed out the table console to Derec in case he had a use for it. He really didn't, finding that he was able to contact any branch of the computer system on the planet with his mind. This morning he started with the one in Dr. Avery's kitchen.

The entire group, including Mandelbrot, sat at the long table with a real breakfast served by two kitchen robots. It included fresh produce and dishes processed from produce instead of from limited nutrient tanks. Derec and Ariel shared their separate adventures with everyone, then Wolruf and Jeff gave their stories. Since Mandelbrot had been shut down for much of the time they had been separated, he had little to tell.

When the anecdotes had ended, Derec sat at the head of the table in an upbeat mood, thinking over his new responsibilities.

"I guess I can have the central computer worry about the particulars of what I have to do," he mused. "If I instruct the central computer to return all the robots to their normal duties, it will do all the organization itself."

"But you can really control it with your mind?" Ariel asked. "And you can program robots mentally, too?"

"Apparently I can. I'm still getting used to the idea myself."

"To all your human attributes," said Mandelbrot, "you have now added some of the advantages of a robot."

Jeff laughed. "Without the liabilities, if you know what I mean." He winked.

While the others laughed, Derec was aware of a message in his mind from the central computer, answering a question he had posed.

"NO EVIDENCE OF DR. AVERY ON THE PLANET HAS BEEN REPORTED," said the central computer.

If Dr. Avery was here at all, Derec realized, he now had all the disadvantages they had had while on the run from him. They now had all the resources he had used. Even more, considering that they were not burdened by insanity.

Considering Dr. Avery's paranoia, Derec felt certain that he had left the planet. Maybe he had gone home to Aurora. Perhaps he had returned to his apartment on Earth, or had other hideaways in reserve, as well.

"Thank 'u," said Wolruf. "Good brreakfasst. Could sleep morr now."

"I believe we can locate comfortable sleeping rooms here," said Mandelbrot. "The luxury of this room and this meal imply similar luxury elsewhere in this residence."

"I'll find a way to shut down the booby-traps and riddles," said Derec, grinning at Ariel.

She laughed. "It's hard to believe. For the first time, Robot City will be at peace, running smoothly, and no longer full of mystery."

"And you have plenty of Keys to Perihelion with which to travel," said Mandelbrot. "Perhaps Wolruf can be sent home."

She shrugged her caninoid shoulders. "Resst first."

"I wonder what kind of shape the ship is in," said Jeff. "I only rented it."

"Don't worry," said Derec. "I'll have the *Minneapolis* fully repaired, cleaned, polished, and outfitted for you. We're more than square for any debt you felt you owed us. But you're welcome to stay as long as you want."

"Thanks," said Jeff. He shook his head, grinning. "Robot City. It's never been a dull town."

When everyone had finished breakfast, Jeff and Wolruf excused themselves to accompany Mandelbrot in further exploration of Dr. Avery's immense quarters.

Later, after function robots had cleared the table and Derec and Ariel were alone in the great hall, he stood gazing into the fire that continued to blaze. He still felt melancholy.

"Is something wrong?" Ariel asked quietly.

"Oh . . . I was just thinking about Dr. Avery. How his wonderful plans got all twisted. And how after researching cultures with Professor Leong and all, he just seemed to drop that subject after a certain point. He is obviously a brilliant man, yet he threw so much away." He looked up at her. "I found out something, too."

"What?"

"I'm not sure we stopped him in time after all. From what I can get out of the central computer, I think some of the robots may have launched themselves from their assembly points before I cancelled that instruction."

Ariel drew in a quick breath. "If that's true, then they will be building more Robot Cities, just as Dr. Avery wanted. And who knows what precise orders he gave them?"

"I may be able to find that out in the computer," said Derec. "Maybe I can even call them back somehow; I won't know till I spend some time on it. But there's something else."

"What? What's wrong?"

"I have my identity back, but . . . I still have amnesia. I don't have all my memory back." He turned to look at her. "Finding my father wasn't exactly constructive."

"Maybe you could . . . oh, I don't know. Perhaps locating your mother would help. Or some of the Avery robots might know of a way to help. Just think how much help you might get from Robot City and even the robots that may have left."

Derec nodded. "I haven't given up. Don't worry about that." He grinned. "That isn't me. And from what I've seen, it isn't you, either."

"It certainly isn't . . . David."

Ariel laughed, looked into his eyes, and tossed her hair back. On an impulse, he slid his arms around her waist and drew her close. Then he kissed her waiting lips and felt her arms tighten around his neck.

Isaac Asimov's Robot City continues with *Robot City #7*, in which Derec is summoned to a distant planet and encounters a robotic experiment fantastically different from anything he has seen on Robot City.

DATA BANK

CARGO ROBOT: Not all of the robots of Robot City are positronic in nature. Many of those whose jobs are especially simple have been equipped with brains that are more like computers than like robot brains. These function robots are analogous to the tools used by positronic robots. They are incapable of real thought; they are also not bound by the Three Laws of Robotics.

The cargo robot is one example of a non-positronic function robot. Programmed with a map of Robot City and its transport systems, it is essentially a container that can load and unload itself and move along preset paths. It has just enough intelligence to avoid obstacles and decide which cargoes should be loaded in the internal compartment and which should be carried on the forklift-like arms.

Illustrations by Paul Rivoche

COURIER ROBOT: Another function robot is the courier. Smaller than a cargo robot, it is faster and more maneuverable. Since all mail in Robot City—in fact, all communications except face-to-face speech—is routed electronically through the main computer, the courier robot's primary job is the delivery of tools and unique artifacts.

Like the cargo robot, the courier robot's lack of positronic intelligence makes it an optional means of covert transportation, since it cannot recognize when it is being used as such.

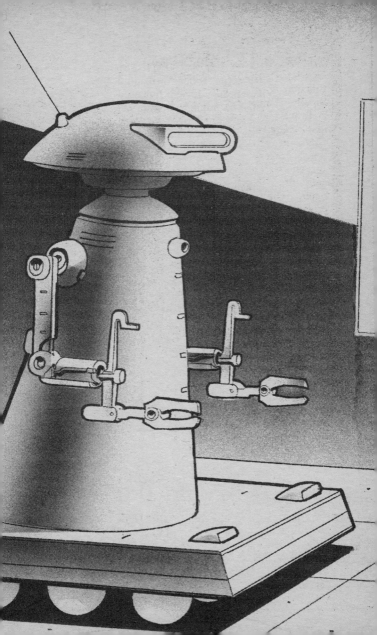

OBSERVATION ROBOT: The observation robot is a reading and recording device. It is used mostly for taking inventories, where it will simply take down the serial numbers of collections of objects (such as robots awaiting repair) and report the details to the positronic robot commanding it. In such cases, it is programmed with the location of the serial number. It can also be used in quality control and diagnosis, though. When it is doing that, it is programmed with an image of the correct appearance of the object under consideration, and it records and reports any discrepancies.

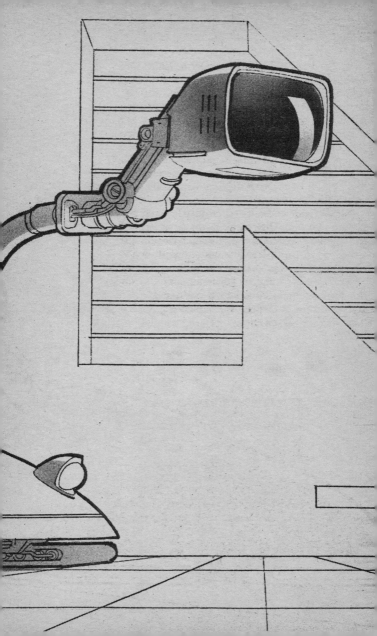

PRIORITY 4 REGIONAL CONTIN-GENCY POWER STATION: The major source of energy for Robot City is the fusion pack. One small micropack can power an industrial robot for over a year before needing to be replaced or refueled; a series of larger packs can provide all the necessary energy for a part of a city. Although fusion packs are extremely safe and reliable, the First Law has compelled the robot Supervisors of Robot City to allow for the possibility of a power failure.

Should the centrally controlled power system of Robot City break down, a series of regional contingency power stations would come on line. Although the goal of the designers was to make any shift in power sources undetectably smooth to human inhabitants, it was necessary to assign priorities to different areas of the city. This station serves a high-priority neighborhood.

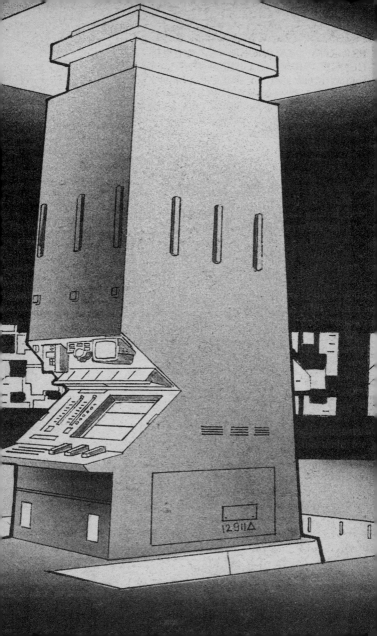

THE *MINNEAPOLIS*: Most interstellar ships are clumsy, at best, once they reach a planetary atmosphere. They are capable of landing very gently at prepared spaceports, but in an emergency they are likely to hit the surface with a noticeable impact. The Hayashi-Smith Space/Shuttle model, however, has complete ground-to-space capability.

In deep space the *Minneapolis* uses a standard hyperdrive. Within solar systems, she maneuvers with normal impulse engines. However, she can also fly within an atmosphere, making use of an aerodynamic design and ramjet engines. This makes it possible for her to put down safely on any sufficiently long, flat surface.

In shuttle mode, the interior of the *Minneapolis* is usually set up with seating for ten. The cabin can be rearranged, however, so that each seat becomes a bunk. This is not a luxurious arrangement for longer (that is, interstellar) trips, but it is satisfactory.

DR. AVERY'S LAIR: Deep beneath the surface of Robot City, Dr. Avery's hidden refuge is a reflection of his own psychology. Inspired, secretive, confusing and confused, and utterly mad, it is a maze of the symbols and themes that form his obsessions.

Some of the rooms take the shape of the Key to Perihelion; others are decorated with the shape. Many of the objects that are scattered through the complex of rooms come from cultures that represent permanence and persistence to Dr. Avery.

The weird shapes of some of the rooms, and the mixtures of ancient and modern, purely decorative and strictly utilitarian, even the echoes in some of the collected objects of Circuit Breaker, all are signs of the infolding of a great architect's mind. As his consciousness descended into obsession and paranoia, he withdrew into the maze-like warren of his hideaway.

WILLIAM F. WU

William F. Wu is a five-time nominee for the Hugo, Nebula, and World Fantasy Awards. He is the author of the novel *Master Play*, about computer wargamers for hire, and he has had short fiction published in most of the magazines and many anthologies in the field of science fiction and fantasy, including a series of collaborations with Rob Chilson in *Analog*. He is also the author of *Robot City 3: Cyborg*. His short story, "Wong's Lost and Found Emporium," was adapted into an episode of the new *Twilight Zone* television show in 1985 and his first published story, "By the Flicker of the One-Eyed Flame," was adapted and performed on stage in 1977. He holds a Ph.D. in American Culture from the University of Michigan, and is married to fantasy artist Diana Gallagher Wu.